Swans in Winter

Also by Kim Antieau

Novels

The Blue Tail

Broken Moon

Church of the Old Mermaids

Coyote Cowgirl

Deathmark

The Fish Wife

Her Frozen Wild

The Gaia Websters

The Jigsaw Woman

Mercy, Unbound

Ruby's Imagine

Nonfiction

Counting on Wildflowers: An Entanglement

The Salmon Mysteries: A Guidebook to a Reimagining of the Eleusinian Mysteries

Short Stories

The First Book of Old Mermaids Tales

Trudging to Eden

Chapbook

Blossoms

Blog

www.kimantieau.com

SWANS
IN
WINTER

KIM ANTIEAU

Ruby Rose's Fairy Tale Emporium • 2012

Swans in Winter
by Kim Antieau

Copyright © 2012 by Kim Antieau

ISBN-13: 978-1467920957
ISBN-10: 1467920959

Cover photo by Tommason | Dreamstime.com.
Book design by Mario Milosevic.
Special thanks to Nancy Milosevic and Ruth Ford Biersdorf.

Electronic editions of this book are
available at most ebook stores

A production of
Ruby Rose's Fairy Tale Emporium
Published by Green Snake Publishing
www.greensnakepublishing.com

www.kimantieau.com

for all that is mythic and wild,
and for the women of Skamania
who love the land,
and especially for Betty P.,
who created the original POOL

CHAPTER ONE

THE AUTUMN RAIN tasted like cloud sweat. India leaned against the cottonwood for protection from the icy east wind and stood on her toes to see over the tall dirty-gold pond grass. A white neck curving to gray floated into view. India grinned and put her hand over her mouth so she would not laugh out loud.

The swans were back!

The swan wiped her black beak on her white and gray neck. Then she stopped. Another swan floated into view. They both looked at India. Talking to each other about the strange watching creature? India wondered.

Another swan joined them.

India stepped forward until she could see most of the east end of Turtle Pond.

Four, five, six swans, she counted.

Gracefully, the swans glided west, away from her, elegant S curves. India wanted to dance a jig or sing a song. Twenty-seven swans!

She gasped. They were so beautiful.

Being this close to the swans made India feel like she was in the midst of a miracle. Or a fairy tale where the hera has just discovered the treasure—or the answer to the riddle of life.

Suddenly, all as one, the swans pumped their wings and lifted up from the pond, no splashes or cries of distress like the ducks, no annoyed honking like the geese. Just air. Silence. Then their own peculiar song of . . . jubilance? Irritation? What was that sound? How could she describe it?

Otherworldly. No. Childlike. Eerie.

India leaned her head back and turned as the swans flew over her. More curves. White fading into the clouds. They became a stark line of white against the dark rocky gorge cliffs as they followed the Columbia River west.

In another moment, India could no longer see them. She looked down again.

She jumped at the sight of a man standing twenty feet from her. He stared after the swans, too. Bearded. Head covered with a black cap. Dressed in an orange parka. A hunter? No gun. Boots muddy.

India started to walk away.

"Did you notice how many?" the man asked.

India turned around. The rain had stopped, the wind lessened.

Kim Antieau

"Twenty-seven," she said.

The man reached into his parka, pulled out a small spiral notebook with a tiny pen attached to it. He unhooked the pen, wrote something in the pad, then shoved them both into his pocket again.

"Thanks," he said. "I got up late today." He nodded toward the river.

India followed the tilt of his head and saw a small blue tent in the distance. He was going to freeze or drown if that tent was his only shelter.

"You're the guy Jack Combs from the reserve told me about," India said. "You're studying the swans this winter."

The man nodded. "That's me," he said. He looked her in the eyes and smiled. Why was he looking so intently at her? She wanted to step away from his gaze.

He held out his hand.

Oh no, she thought, now I have to touch him!

"Benjamin Swan."

"You're kidding," she said, shaking his hand. He held on to her hand for a second too long.

"Yes, that's my name," he said, laughing. "It's worse. My middle name is Anthony." He looked at her expectantly.

"I don't get it," she said.

"Benjamin Anthony Swan. B. A. Swan."

"Your parents had a sense of humor."

He nodded and still watched her. She looked away. She had a pot of minestrone on the stove. A paperback mystery waited. And she was cold.

"You like the swans," he said.

She glanced at him. "Yes."

They both looked at the pond, now empty of swans.

"I figure a world where swans exist can't be all bad," India said.

"Thank you," he said.

India looked at the man. "What? Oh, yes, well, I meant the feathered kind."

"Ahhh," he said.

"It was nice meeting you," India said.

"But I haven't met you," he said. He smiled. His beard was black and brown. Any gray? India instinctively touched her own covered head. Hers was nearly all gray. She was the only forty-something woman she knew who did not dye her hair. Gray is beautiful she told her friends; I've earned every one of these gray hairs. They laughed at her and said, gray is just old. They were right, of course. As India's hair turned from brown to gray, people stopped seeing her. It was as if she no longer existed. Strangers looked right through her.

Until now. This stranger kept looking right at her. What was wrong with him?

"You're India, aren't you?" he asked. "Jack told me about you, too."

"Oh? What'd he say, be on the lookout for the little old lady who haunts the meadow by Turtle Pond?"

The man flinched.

Feeling a little bitter these days, girl? she thought. Gawd. She wanted to get out of this conversation gracefully.

"No, he said his friend India lived nearby and she knows a lot about ponds."

"That's me," she said. "I'm India." She was embarrassed. "But I think Jack must have been pulling your leg. Perhaps he said I knew a lot about lakes, not ponds. Because that's my name. India Lake. He's always teasing me about my name. My parents had a sense of humor, too." Why was she babbling like this? "Well, my lunch is waiting. I better go."

She waved, turned, and hurried away. What was wrong with her? She was with the public nearly every day. Why was she suddenly a raving lunatic?

"I like it," the man called.

India looked over her shoulder as she kept walking.

"What?"

"Your name. I like your name, India Lake. It's geographical."

She stopped. "Geographical?"

"Yeah, geography. A place you can call home. India Lake."

Rain began pelting India. The wind shook what leaves were left on the cottonwood. Benjamin Swan stood in the pasture between the pond and the cottonwood, feet apart, anchored in the muddy ground, dressed in his bright orange parka. He grinned at her.

She smiled uncomfortably, frowned, then turned away. The rain was cold. She wished she could fly home.

Instead, she ran.

INDIA GOT TO the front porch of her little gray rented

house seconds before the clouds burst open. She glanced at the gorge cliffs across the river. Snow fell there, dusting the evergreens with what looked like powdered sugar and falling into ravines, creating white Vs that would remain until spring.

India went inside and shook off her wet coat, hat, scarf, boots, and socks. Her slacks were wet, too. She stepped out of them and took the whole pile of clothes to the laundry room where she spread them out to dry. She got another pair of slacks from the chair in her bedroom. She stood in front of the picture window holding her slacks and looking out at the storm.

The rain fell in sheets over the river and out in the meadow where she had just talked with the man about the swans. She could see part of the pond from here, the curves of its banks serpentine. The first time she had seen the pond she had assumed it was this murky little place where nothing lived. Until Rhonda told her about the turtles. Then India took her binoculars out to the edge of the muddy water and looked through them until she saw turtles sunning themselves on the shiny gray trunks of long ago dead and decapitated trees.

Each time India returned to the pond she saw more wildlife: the great blue heron fishing at the edges, bald eagles swooping quietly down from a nearby cottonwood, osprey noisily searching for prey in the cloudy waters, various species of ducks raising their young, and kingfishers calling out as they furiously flapped their wings and flew over the pond. During the summer India watched the female turtles go into a kind of trance as they laid their eggs along the sides of the path; she waited until fall to watch them hatch out.

When Jack Combs, the ranger, rented the state land surrounding the pond to a cattle rancher who was also the local sheriff, things changed. India fought to keep them from mowing or driving along the path when the turtles were laying eggs. She called the sheriff each time the cows broke through the fencing and headed straight for the pond, where they trampled the fragile shoreline as they grazed and defecated. The rancher told her, "Turtles are nasty creatures. I've seen turtles swoop underneath a baby duck and pull it right down into the water and drown it."

"Those are snapping turtles; these are western pond turtles," she explained to him, although that was beside the point.

India told Rhonda, "I should have said so what? Are we only supposed to save those things that are cute and cuddly? What a boring world that would be."

Now India looked away from the pond and tried to find the blue tent. She could not see it. She hoped Benjamin Swan didn't freeze. She pulled on her slacks and wondered if someone outside could see her inside, half naked, trying to get dressed.

She shrugged and padded into the bathroom and looked at her reflection in the mirror. Her curly gray hair was matted down on one side. Bags under her eyes. Blue eyes. Not as blue as Benjamin Swan's. She shook her head. She had never been vain before. Why start now? She stared at her reflection. She hadn't been vain before because she had been attractive most of her life. Pretty. Cute.

She was long past cute.

It made her angry that she cared.

She stuck out her tongue at her reflection, then went into the kitchen to heat up her soup.

It was all nonsense. She did not like thinking about herself in those terms: attractive, ugly, old, young. Her life had never been about those things. Why had she become aware of it lately?

She ladled the minestrone into an apricot-colored fiesta ware bowl and went and sat at the round wooden table in front of the picture window. Rain streaked the glass, making the outside world look like a melting painting.

India heard a knock at her front door.

"Hello!" Rhonda's voice.

"Come in," India called. She looked across the room as Rhonda opened the door, shut it, and took off her coat.

"Geez Louise," Rhonda said. "It is cold and miserable." She strode across the room. She was a big older woman with the grace of a flamingo. Or a swan. No. A bear. A big ol' Grizzly bear.

"Minestrone on the stove," India said as Rhonda pulled out a chair.

"I don't want any of your healthy crap," Rhonda said, grinning. "What are you up to today?"

"Went out to the pond," India said between mouthfuls. Steam rose from the concoction of zucchinis, peas, potatoes, carrots, onion, celery, garlic, and a bit of tomato and pasta. How could anyone not want to fill their bellies with this delicious brew?

"This is so good, Rhonda. You don't know what you're missing."

"That's what you said about that tofu broccoli casserole," she said.

"Yeah and I was right," India said. "You would have liked it if I'd said the tofu was fried chicken bits. Besides, I only gave you some because you insisted on tasting it."

"Well, I've learned my lesson," Rhonda said. She shuddered. India laughed.

"I saw a tent out between the meadow and the river," Rhonda said. "You hear anything about who the occupant is?"

"He's a friend of Jack Combs," India said. "He's studying the swans."

"He's actually sleeping in that tent?"

"I didn't ask."

"You met him?"

"Yeah, he was out counting the swans. Get this. His name is Benjamin Swan."

"How apropos," Rhonda said. "How does Jack know him?"

"I don't know."

Rhonda rolled her eyes. "Where's the whole story here, girl? You're the librarian. Aren't you supposed to be an information specialist? This is very little information, my friend. Isaac and I should have him over for dinner. Was he interesting?"

India shrugged. "He seemed nice enough."

Rhonda looked at her. "But?"

"No but. He was nice. He'd fit in at one of your dinners, I'm sure."

"One of *our* dinners? What does that mean?" Rhonda asked.

"It means you find the most interesting people in the area and invite them to dinner so you can interrogate them about their lives," India said. "He'd probably have lots of interesting conversation in him, and he could use a hot meal." India pushed away her empty bowl. "He stared at me a little. Made me a little bit uncomfortable."

"Psycho-uncomfortable?"

"No, I don't think so. I shouldn't have said anything. I'm sure he's nice."

India stood, picked up the bowl, and carried it to the sink.

"Have you decided where you're going on your vacation?" Rhonda asked. "When's it start?"

India returned to the table and sat next to Rhonda.

"In a couple of days. December first. I don't know if I'm going anywhere. Maybe I'll stay here and write, paint, watch the swans."

Rhonda made a noise. "This is the worst time of the year to stay here. You need sunshine, a bathing suit, someone tall, dark, and handsome."

India laughed. "Yeah, that's what I need. You think everything can be solved with sex."

"No, I just fantasize everything can be solved with sex. I'm an old lady. I got no more desire."

"Right. I see you and Isaac making out when you think no one is looking." India laughed and affectionately slapped Rhonda's arm. "What'd you come over for anyway? I've got things to do. I can't waste my afternoon gabbing with you."

"I was taking a stroll," Rhonda said, "and I saw the swans flying overhead. I wanted to let you know they were back. And to see if you wanted to sign up for the belly dancing class on Tuesday. Violet needs one more to make the class go."

"I've told you before I've never been good at organized dance. I am not graceful."

"Come on. It's supposed to be a very ancient form of dance. The body creates geometric shapes that heal, make desire, and create the Universe. Dance existed before sound, you know. Before the word."

"I thought the purpose of belly dancing was to get men hot," India said.

"No, it's to get women hot."

"Violet tell you all this?" India asked.

"No," Rhonda said. "Please. Violet is a baby. But she's a good instructor."

"All right," India said. "I'll go to one class and see."

"Good. Will you give me a ride?"

India laughed. "Of course."

"Wear something sexy to class," Rhonda said as she stood. "I want to see some skin."

"I'll see if I have any."

"Skin?"

"Something sexy. Now go home."

"I love how gracious you are," Rhonda said. She kissed India's forehead. "See you later, gator."

Kim Antieau

CHAPTER TWO

INDIA STOOD AT the circulation desk. It was a busy afternoon. The kids had early release from school and now crowded the library. Normally India liked the library busy, but today she felt off. It was her last day for two months, yet it seemed like any other day. No cards from her staff. No cake. Of course, they knew she wouldn't eat cake, so maybe they figured it was a waste of time. Still.

She heard laughter and looked at a table of preadolescent boys hunched over a pile of magazines. She smiled. She wanted people to be comfortable. It was their library, after all. She liked working here because she could have easy superficial relationships with people. She was social all day and then went home by herself.

Things were changing, though. She glanced at the internet stations and catalog terminals. Out in the public part of the building she counted thirteen different computer terminals. The computers were fast, and they helped her find what patrons needed quicker than she had been able to before, but people were impatient now; they demanded and expected information fast, faster, fastest. Every day the software changed. She could not always keep up and neither could her patrons. Sometimes she felt like one of those people who had been alive when the world changed from candles to electricity and horse and buggy to automobiles. She was not sure where she belonged.

She was tired of everyone being irritated all of the time. The patrons were demanding and irritated; her staff was angry and irritated that they had to deal with the ever-changing computer world and the demanding, irritated—and irritating—patrons. Recently India had yelled at a patron. Screamed at him, really. It had been at the end of a long tiring day, and she had not been able to maintain her "public servant" voice after listening to the patron berate her for five minutes because the internet was down. Soon after their "argument" the man complained to the main office, and India's supervisor in Vancouver called and reminded her that she had over two months of vacation time accrued, and it was time to take some.

"I'm going on break," Teri said, coming up behind India. "All these kids are getting on my last nerve."

India nodded. India was the only one on staff who did not have children—and she was the only one who could tolerate a library full of pre-pubescent and teenaged children. She walked across the room to get an empty book cart. The boys giggled as she went by. She had known most of them since they were babies. As she returned with the cart, one of the boys whispered, "She's a lesbo, you know."

India stopped and leaned down until her head was level with theirs. She said loudly, "Lesbos is an island, boys, where women devoted to the goddesses Artemis and Aphrodite went to practice the art of *charis*."

"Huh?" one of the boys said.

"*Charis*. It means grace. The graces: art, dancing, poetry, music, love. I think the word you were groping for, as it were, is lesbian." Her voice rose even higher when she said lesbian. "And I wish I were a lesbian, so I could go live on Lesbos or some tropical island where there were only women and I wouldn't have to deal with snot-faced little boys like you."

The boys giggled. She scooped up their magazines.

"And Jeff, you better be nice to me. I saw you minutes after you dropped from your momma's womb, and I seem to remember a certain birthmark on your—well, you know where. Shall I describe it?"

"Ohhhh!" the boys squealed.

India winked and walked back to the circulation desk. Jack Combs leaned against the counter.

"You're cruel," Jack said.

India smiled. "Hey, I'm tired of people thinking I'm harmless. Those boys need to show some respect. Or at the very least they should be terrified of me. You know his mother would back me up."

"Reminded me of the old you," Jack said.

"The old me? What's that supposed to mean?"

Jack cleared his throat. "Nothing. Just the good ol' days when you were a happy smart-ass."

India raised her eyebrows, then said, "What are you doing in town all dressed up in your park ranger duds?"

"Talking with the commissioners about next spring," Jack said. "They want me to let them spray Franz Lake for mosquitoes. I told them I wouldn't unless it's a health crisis. Same ol' crap."

"You held your ground," India said. "Good for you. You're the only one who's getting paid to protect our interests who actually protects our interests. At least most of the time. We don't need to mention the cows and barbed wire fences again. None of the other county officials care about the environment."

Jack smiled wanly. They had had this conversation many times before.

"Hey, Benjamin told me you two met."

"Yeah," India said, waiting to hear that Benjamin had labeled her as a local loony.

Jack nodded and stared at the papers on the circulation desk. India wondered when Jack had stopped looking at her—really looking at her.

"Is he sleeping in that tent?" India asked.

"He will until it gets too cold," Jack said. "I've offered him a room at my place or that mobile home next door. He got a grant to do this, did I tell you?" He glanced at her. India looked at his eyes. Brown. Deep dark brown.

Kim Antieau

He used to look at her. Back when they were dating regularly. That was a long time ago. Now they were good friends, the kind of close friends only former lovers could be. Well, not exactly former. Secret lovers?

"India," Jack said. "Is everything all right?"

"What? Oh, I'm sorry." She dropped her gaze from his eyes. "I was lost in thought. You want to come over tonight?"

"Can't," he said, slapping the countertop.

"Got plans?"

"Yep." He didn't look at her, only smiled a lopsided grin. He had a date.

"Have fun," India said. "I better get some work done." She walked out from behind the circulation desk.

"If I get back early I could come over," Jack offered as India walked away.

She wanted to say something cruel. Instead she called over her shoulder, "No. Go have a good time."

Teri sat in the workroom flipping through a magazine.

"I think I'm done," India said.

Teri looked up. "Your replacement librarian won't be here until tomorrow."

India smiled grimly. "You can survive for another thirty minutes."

"Yeah, but—"

"Is there any reason I need to stay?" India asked as she got her coat and purse from the coat tree.

"I have five more minutes on my break."

India sighed. "I'll wait then."

She carried her coat and purse out to the circulation desk. She was sick and tired of this place and all of its petty little rules and regulations. Couldn't Teri see she *had* to leave, she had to get away?

India closed her eyes and breathed deeply.

Why did she have to get away? Because Jack going on a date hurt her feelings? She had wanted him to date someone else for years. She was always trying to fix him up. After all, they were friends who occasionally saw each other naked. Comfortable for her and him, she thought.

She opened her eyes. Benjamin Swan was standing in front of her. This time his hat was off. His hair was raven black. No gray.

"Hello," she said.

"Hello, India Lake," he said.

She grimaced. When Benjamin Swan said it, her name sounded like a line out of a country western song.

"Hello, Benjamin Swan."

He smiled. "You remember me."

"Of course. What can I do for you?" she asked in her helpful librarian voice.

"My truck broke down," he said. "I wondered if you could give me a lift home. Jack is staying in town for a while."

"So I heard," India said. "Home? You mean that tent? I read it's going to freeze tonight."

"It's plenty warm," he said. "Besides, I can always go over to Jack's."

"How? You haven't a truck."

Teri came out of the workroom. India put on her coat and picked up her purse from the circulation desk.

"I'll see you in a couple of months," India said to Teri. "Have fun." She looked at Benjamin. "Sure, come on. I'll take you home."

They went outside into the near night. India unlocked the passenger door of her blue Honda, then went around, opened her door, and slid inside. She started up the car, then rubbed her hands together. Benjamin Swan seemed to fill up her tiny car.

"It'll warm up fast," she said.

"I'm fine."

"Today was my last day," she said. She turned on the headlights and shifted the car into first. They drove away from the library and out onto State Route 14.

"You've quit?"

"No. I accumulated too much vacation time. They told me to use it or lose it. So I'm taking it all at once."

She sped up as they left the town limits. The stars were beginning to come out one at a time, as if someone were slowly poking tiny holes in a huge blue-black stage curtain.

India glanced at Benjamin. He gazed out the window.

"How's the swan study going?" India asked.

"Fine," he said. "I'm starting to distinguish one swan from another. At least I think I am."

"You've done this before? You're a naturalist?"

"Amateur. I've volunteered for projects like this before," he said. "Jack told me they needed someone here so I applied for a grant. Jack's been great. Of course he says he didn't mean for me to sleep outside in a tent, but I want to know if I can do it."

"How long have you been out there?"

"Ten days."

India shook her head. "I've never been a good camper. I grew up out in the country and saw myself as Nature's child, but out in the woods in a tent, I got cold. It was embarrassing."

"I have to admit I've been pretty cold these last couple of nights."

India laughed. "I bet."

The road curved past Beacon Rock, the core of an ancient volcano that now served as a tourist attraction.

"One day I couldn't sleep so I walked to Beacon Rock and climbed to the top. It was incredible."

"Wow. Weren't you scared?"

"Of what?" Benjamin asked.

"I don't know. Of slipping. Of a cougar eating you. Of falling to your death."

"I thought I would be," he said. "I don't like taking risks much. But this felt right. I went the back way, through the cow pastures, so I wasn't on 14 for very long. I saw deer and a coyote. Heard an owl. I saw the reflection of the moon in the river. Just beautiful."

India was sorry she had missed it. "Would you like to have some soup at my house before you go back to your tent?"

She turned the car off 14, went across the railroad tracks, and down Shore Drive.

"Thanks, but Rhonda and Isaac invited me over for dinner."

"Oh. OK. Shall I drop you at their house?"

"No, right here is fine. I need to change my clothes."

She stopped the car at the entrance to the meadow next to the pond. Benjamin pulled a flashlight from his pocket, then looked at India.

"I hope you come out to see the swans," he said. "I would enjoy talking with you."

"Now that I'm off work, I'll probably be out there every day," she said.

Benjamin got out of the car. India watched the flashlight beacon bob up and down as he walked away.

She wondered how he was able to change clothes inside that tiny tent.

"Strange bird," she said, then laughed at herself.

She drove home. It was dark and cold inside her house. She turned the light on and the heat up. She checked her messages. Rhonda had invited her to dinner.

"I guess that means I can't totally feel sorry for myself," she said.

She curled up on the couch and dragged a quilt across herself. She closed her eyes.

"Just for a minute," she whispered.

SHE STARTED AWAKE to someone knocking at her door. She threw off the quilt and jumped up.

"Who is it?" she asked, feeling totally disoriented.

"Benjamin Swan."

"Didn't I just drop you off?"

"That was two hours ago."

She opened the door. Benjamin was dressed in a black jacket, black T-shirt, and blue jeans. No orange parka. She blinked.

"Rhonda asked me to come get you before dinner gets cold."

"Come in, come in," India said, motioning Benjamin into the house. She shut the door behind him.

"Who's their company?"

"Some friends from California. One's in the movie biz. Another's a lawyer."

India rubbed her arms. "I'm not sure I'm up to all that tonight. I don't feel very interesting right now. She only invites you if she thinks you're interesting."

"I have strict instructions to bring you back with me," Benjamin said.

"Do you always do what people tell you to do?"

"Just women," Benjamin said. "I obey wisdom."

India laughed. "Yeah, well, I'm too tired. I don't feel like socializing or any of that." She wanted to stomp her foot but decided that was a little too juvenile.

"Let me show you something that will make you feel better. If you still don't want to go after that, I'll return to Rhonda's empty handed, so to speak, and take my punishment like the coward I am. All right? Get dressed. Warm. It's really cold out."

"Aye-aye," India said.

She went to her bedroom, took off her work clothes and pulled on her winter pants, shirt, and sweatshirt. Then she returned to the living room and bundled up in her coat, scarf, hat, gloves, socks, and boots.

"Call me Nanook of the North," she said. She got her keys and they stepped into a cold clear night. The stars glittered. The air smelled like snow.

India followed Benjamin down the road, across the narrow bridge, and down the lane into the meadow. They walked until they were in complete darkness. India blinked, waiting for her eyes to adjust. She saw porch lights across the river, tiny beacons of home. Their feet crunched over the gravel. Then they were on grass, walking into the cow pasture and toward the cottonwood tree.

Benjamin took India's gloved hand—for an instant— to lead her to the dip in the Earth where she could not see the pond and the occupants of the pond presumably could not see her. He put a finger to his lips. India listened. At first she heard only the ringing in her ears. Then the traffic a mile across the river.

Then a cooing sound. Lots of cooing. Only that was not the right word. Comforting noises. Ooooh. Oooo. All together it was almost like chortling. Gentle easy laughter.

The swans were singing.

India looked at Benjamin and grinned. He smiled and held out his hand. She took it and twirled around once, dancing to the sound of the swans easing each other to rest. Benjamin did the same.

Then India let go of his hand, and they left the swans and headed for Rhonda's and Isaac's with the secret of their swan dance safe between them.

CHAPTER THREE

INDIA STOOD IN the dip in the meadow, high enough up the slope to see the swans but not close enough to frighten them into flight. She watched a gray-necked swan preen. An adult swan spread out her wings.

"Magnificent," India whispered.

Several dug around in the mud for wapato.

"Good morning."

India turned and saw Benjamin.

"Hello," she whispered. "No swan songs this morning. They're pretty quiet."

Benjamin nodded. "Some people still believe swans break out into glorious song when they die," Benjamin said. "Four thousand whistling swans were killed in the United States at one time in an attempt to prove or disprove this theory."

"That's awful," India said.

Two swans slid their heads and neck up against the other, their bills facing Benjamin and India.

"Looks like they're cuddling," India said. "I've heard they mate for life."

"Some do, some don't," Benjamin said, "though it's believed the majority do. A pair doesn't actually make a nest and lay eggs until they're about four or five years old, but they go steady for a couple of years before that."

India laughed. "Go steady? Is that swan vernacular?"

A great blue heron squawked, then lifted up from the pond. India and Benjamin walked to the cottonwood—away from the water—so the swans could have more room, in case the heron's jitters spooked them. The big cranky honked once more as it flew out over the river.

"Did you stay very late at Rhonda's last night?" India asked.

"I spent the night," Benjamin said.

India laughed.

"It was cold last night," he said.

India covered her mouth, so the birds would not hear her laughing.

"I thought you were a mountain man," she said.

"Hardly. Did you have a good time last night?" He was watching her again, as he had last night. Every time India looked up, Benjamin's gaze had been on her.

India shrugged. "I love Rhonda and Isaac, and I enjoy their friends for the most part, but I often feel like a pet dog they pay attention to for a little while before they move on to important things. I finally figured out I'm a baby to them and their friends. I'm too young to know anything. Then in town at work, I'm too old to know anything. It's a delicate age." India laughed. "When I first moved here, I would walk around the neighborhood. Rhonda told me later she would see me and think I was this quiet nothing. Then she heard me give a talk at the library about writing. She said before that she assumed I was this demure brainless twit."

"Really? She told you that?"

"Sure. That's why I like her. She doesn't hide stuff. You know what's what. She meant no malice. Do you want to walk so we can keep warm?"

Benjamin nodded. They walked up the slope, then through the gate to the next pasture, skirting the mud puddles until they walked on grass again. A red-tailed hawk called out a warning.

"One," India said.

Called out again.

"Two," Benjamin said.

The hawk took off from the dead top of one of the old cottonwoods.

"I can't fly," India called. "I don't eat meat! You could have stayed put."

Benjamin laughed.

"There used to be a Native village here," India said. "I'm not sure exactly where, but in this general area. Homesteaders came later. That old house up by the rail-road tracks belonged to one of the grandchildren of the homesteaders."

They followed the cow path into a small wood of evergreens.

"Before the cows came, the ground cover here was all chickweed," India said. "I would just sit here and graze. Sweet delicious chickweed. It was like a little fairy land. Whenever I find chickweed I'm certain fairies are not far behind."

"The Celts believed swans were fairy women," Benjamin said.

India nodded. "Ahh, so I was right. This is—or was—a fairy land. Now you can see all that is left of the chickweed patch is cow shit. And the meadow is full of thistle where it wasn't before. The cows eat, they shit, and the seeds in their shit grow. Or seeds land on their shit and grow, I'm not sure which. In any case, they spread noxious weeds. Then the ranchers come in and demand the government spray pesticides to get rid of the weeds. It's a vicious cycle. I fought Jack every step of the way, but they let the cows come anyway. Plus the cows keep getting out near the pond. The entire ecology of the pond is different. There aren't as many turtles. The water is gray. Way too many geese."

"Any upside to the cows?"

India and Benjamin walked amongst the trees. India's fingers traced the grooves in the black bark of one tree.

"No. Well, the swans didn't come here before the cows, but I'm not crediting the cows with that. That is coincidence. I know that I brought the swans here."

"I don't doubt it," Benjamin said, "but how did you accomplish this extraordinary feat?"

India smiled. "I wanted to write a story about the swans, but I wanted to set it here on the pond instead of Franz Lake. I have to drive to Franz Lake, plus there's no where to watch the swans except from that pullout along SR14. Anyway, that winter the swans first came here. My story called them here."

"Did you write the story?"

"I started it, but it didn't work out."

"Jack said you'd had a book published."

"Doesn't he have anything better to talk about than me?" India asked.

"Yes, but the other stuff isn't relevant to this conversation."

India laughed. "OK. Well, I used to write. Now I don't much. Look over here. I want to show you something."

India took Benjamin to a large ant hill amidst the trees. The peak of the cinnamon red and gray hill was caved in.

"They're done for the winter," she said, "but you can get an idea of how magnificent it was."

"It's huge," Benjamin said. He squatted next to the ant hill. "I've never seen anything like this."

"Isn't it beautiful?" India said. "When the ants are here it is an incredible sight. If the sun is full bore on the hill, the few ants move really quickly on the surface of the hill. Because it's so hot, I suppose. I like to stand so that part of my shadow is cast right on the colony. Like my head or hand. The ants pour out of the hill and take the shape of my shadow. I become part of their world. I've always felt protective of ant hills. Most ants are female, you know. Nearly every one you see is a she. Talk about your female wisdom. When I was a girl I found an ant hill out in our woods. I decided to destroy it. I wanted to see what would happen. I planned it. I got up and deliberately went out and kicked it to pieces. Kicked and kicked. I suppose I was angry about something else. All these ants came scurrying out. I saw their panic. I stepped away from my Armageddon and wished I could put it all back. I felt terrible. I started to cry. One of the worse things I ever did in my life."

India stopped. Benjamin was looking up at her.

Why on Earth had she told him that story?

"So that's why I feel protective of ants. In case some other monstrous girl is running about looking for trouble."

Benjamin stood. "Not monstrous. The girl who was you stopped when you realized what you had done. She felt bad. The ants probably rebuilt that hill. Told ant stories about it."

India smiled.

They left the ant hill and walked out of the woods into the open. India glanced at Benjamin. She had not told anyone that story before. Something about Benjamin made her comfortable. And uncomfortable.

"The sun feels nice," Benjamin said.

"Yes."

They stood quietly. India looked toward home. Benjamin stood close to her, and she did not move away.

She should not talk to this man, she thought. She revealed too much about herself. She did not like people to know the details of her life. The sun warmed her face. She shut her eyes for a moment.

"I better go do . . . something," India said. "I've only got eight more weeks to vacate."

They started walking toward the pond. A swan spread her wings again, wide, as if seeking embrace. Or preparing to embrace. Embrace what? Life? Another swan?

"Will you write during your vacation?" Benjamin asked.

"No. I don't think so."

"What about the swan story?"

She shrugged. "It didn't really work out. Though I was thinking of incorporating it into a story about Sasquatch."

"Bigfoot?"

"Yes." They stopped at the green metal gate. India stood on the bottom rail. Thirty or more swans fed at the marshy end of the pond. India heard an occasional swan murmur.

"Bigfoot is a protected species in this county," India said. "Can you believe that? They'll cut down all the trees and spray pesticides everywhere but thirty years or so ago, they declared it a crime to shoot a Sasquatch."

"How did that happen?"

"Apparently there had been a flurry of sightings and some of the experts were saying the only way to prove Sasquatch exists was to kill one," India said. "So all these crackpots converged on the county looking to kill them a Bigfoot. Instead, they kept shooting at each other. The county figured declaring Bigfoot a protected species would save someone's life, beast or not. There was a sighting right here at Beacon Rock just a few years ago."

Benjamin put his left foot up on the bottom rail and leaned against the open gate. "So you believe in Bigfoot?"

"The Native people of this area believe—or once believed—that Sasquatch appears when life is out of balance," India said, dropping down off the gate. "I believe life is out of balance."

"Like the Hopi's Koyaanisqatsi," Benjamin said.

"Yes, exactly. Crazy life. Life that needs another way of living. Life out of balance."

They walked around the gate and mud puddles.

"We are about the only culture that does not believe in fairies or brownies or some *other*," Benjamin said.

"Yes," India said. "I've never seen Sasquatch, but I think we need him or her. They nearly always refer to Bigfoot as a he but if there are baby Bigfeet, they gotta have a momma. Bigfoot may be real or a symbol of the wild. Whichever it is, we need the wild."

"I've heard some strange noises at night here," Benjamin said. "Maybe Bigfoot was checking me out."

"More likely a coyote."

"Or a cricket." Benjamin smiled.

"I'll let you get back to work," India said. "You know, we worry about you out there. Don't freeze to death. I told you I was raised out in the country, but I was never a good camper. I remember at one girl scout camping trip I couldn't sleep because I was so cold. I put on all my clothes, and I was still shivering. I finally got up and went out into the cold to the scout leader's tent to ask for help. She told me to go back to my own tent and live with it. It was my fault, she said, because I had caused so much trouble earlier in the day by scaring the other girls with stories of Green Eyes."

"Green Eyes?"

"This being we kept seeing in the woods. Actually we kept seeing these green eyes. Or talked ourselves into believing that's what we saw. Anyway, the scout leader seemed glad I was miserable. I went back to my tent totally perplexed about what being cold and telling stories had to do with anything. I don't think I ever got to sleep and the incident changed the way I felt about that woman—and myself."

Benjamin watched her again.

"I just told another personal meaningless story. I apologize. I was only trying to tell you not to freeze. If you get too cold, come to my house. I won't tell you you deserve it or that it's your fault."

What was she saying?

"Or you could go to Rhonda's."

She glanced at Benjamin. He was so tall. Big. He could take care of himself. He smiled at her. Such beautiful blue eyes.

"Thank you for your stories," Benjamin said. "I like them."

If she knew him better, she would ask him what he was grinning at.

Oh what the hell.

"What are you grinning at?"

"I can't tell you," Benjamin said. He stood with his feet apart again, as if it he were rooted to the Earth.

"Are you laughing at me?" she asked.

"No, certainly not. I—I—"

"It's all right," India said. "None of my business. See you later, Mr. Swan."

"You, too, India Lake."

INDIA WANDERED FROM room to room in her house. It was so quiet. She stopped at the doorway to her office. She should get a cat or dog. Something. She had not had a pet for a decade or more.

She turned around and returned to the living room. When Raymond left he had taken the cat. India had not wanted her. She told Raymond having a pet was like having a little animal slave. The truth was she did not want the mess. Changing litter boxes. Cat hair everywhere for years even after the cat was gone.

India stood at the picture window and looked out. Was that the real reason? When had she gotten so fastidious?

Maybe it was because she did not want the responsibility. She wanted to come and go as she pleased. Wasn't that why she still rented even though she had lived in the area for a decade?

She looked across the river at the gorge cliffs. The powdery snow had melted, but the white snow Vs remained. Feathery clouds moved west. Some days she stood on the shores of the Columbia River and watched the water flowing west, the clouds directly over the water going east, and the next layer of clouds floating west. A study in wind dynamics—or Zen philosophy. Going with the flow. But which flow?

On a day like today, the gorge was so awesome, so magnificent, that she could not imagine living anywhere else. She felt cradled by the wind-and-water-eroded mountains, soothed by the Columbia River. Sometimes she dreamed the river was red with salmon. Then she would wake up and realize that the true wild salmon were extinct, or nearly so, and she would look out the window and see the haze of pollution that choked the gorge some days. Out here in the Wild West people thought they had the right to burn anything, plus no one had heard of mass transit or car pooling. The result was big city air pollution right out here in the country.

India came from the Midwest. She knew what a place looked like once they had cut down all the trees, fished out the rivers and streams, and killed most of the wildlife: suburbia. In Michigan, she had to drive up north to see the one remaining old growth tree. At least some semblance of wildness remained in the Pacific Northwest. Yet many area residents only valued the wilderness as a cover to give them the privacy to do whatever they wanted out of sight of their neighbors and the government. She had met people who boasted of beating up environmentalists and shooting spotted owls. One neighbor was proud of the fact that he was considered the biggest poacher in the state—he told India this as he tried to steal a turtle from Turtle Pond.

India sat on the couch and pulled the quilt around her.

She had been fighting with these people for so long that sometimes she forgot everyone was not like "them," that everyone was not a "they." She knew a hunter who made fun of her views but always left the woods how he found it, especially since he rarely actually killed anything. She was friends with an independent logger who didn't clear-cut even though his fellow loggers pressured him to do so. There was Rhonda and Isaac. And India's own little environmental group, POOL, and all the women who participated in it.

India rubbed her face. When had she gotten so angry and prejudiced? Old, gray, fastidious, and angry. Pissed Off Old Lady, the real meaning of the acronym POOL.

"As Rhonda would say, 'Geez Louise.'"

She got up and walked to her office door. This time she went inside. She glanced at the shelf that held copies of her published work, including her novel, *Nature Girl*. How long had it been since it came out? Five years? She had thought her dreams were finally coming true when *Nature Girl* was published. She had worked for twenty years to get one of her novels in print.

She pulled the book off the shelf. On the cover was a scantily clad woman stepping into the woods. A little too provocative for the actual story, but she had had no control over what they put on the cover. The reviews of the book had been good, the advertising nil, and the sales mediocre. When she submitted her next novel, her publishers turned it down. So did every other publisher she sent it to. They cited *Nature Girl*'s low sales figures.

When India had first started out, getting published was

the biggest hurdle. Once a writer finally got published, as long as she kept writing good books, the publisher tended to stay with her and help her build an audience, but that was rare nowadays. India put *Nature Girl* back on the shelf. She again felt like one of those people on the cusp of change: She could not seem to keep up. She had more compassion now for people who had to change careers mid-life. She had been writing stories since she was a child. It was her gift. Now, it seemed, no one wanted that gift.

She supposed she needed to learn a new skill. Could you really learn a new gift?

She had made so many plans, had wanted so much in her life. Now she felt useless, unseen, untalented.

Maybe she was like all those old loggers swilling beer at the Spar Tree. They blamed environmentalists because they were out of work. They never acknowledged their own part in their downfall. She wanted to shake them and scream, "You cut down all the trees!" Did people want to shake her and scream some truth to her about her own responsibility in her downfall?

She returned to the living room and looked toward the pond. She spotted Benjamin Swan's orange parka.

Who was he? She rattled on and on when she was with him, yet he said little about himself.

Or maybe she had not listened.

She was so nervous around him.

Wasn't sure why.

Enough of this, she thought.

She had to get dressed for belly dancing class.

CHAPTER FOUR

INDIA DROVE DOWN the block to Rhonda's house. Her friend waited in the dark at the mailbox at the end of her drive. India pushed the passenger door open, and Rhonda got in.

"It's going to be cold tonight," Rhonda said. "Did Benjamin get his truck fixed?"

I didn't see it."

"Brrr."

India continued driving the loop road up to SR14. When the road ended, she pulled out onto the highway.

"I can't believe I let you talk me into this," India said.

"Awww. It'll be fun," Rhonda said. "Remember, it's not only dance, it's geometry."

"Geometry?"

"Sacred geometry. I don't know much about it except it uses shapes and proportions from nature to design buildings, a kind of architectural yoga. We're going to be creating these same shapes with our bodies. Circles. Ss. The symbol for infinity, which is also a kind of serpent shape. We dance these geometric forms, and this movement massages our internal organs and, they say, connects us to the Great Mystery, or to the Great Mother."

"I thought you were an atheist," India said.

"I'm agnostic," Rhonda said. "That means I have no knowledge of the divine. I don't say the divine doesn't exist; I just don't know. It's too big. It's a Great Mystery. If the divine does exist, it would have to be a Great Mother, wouldn't it? In order to handle so many different things. I love Isaac and he can do *one* thing at a time really well, but I never met a man who can do *many* things at once, and do them well. I can cook, eat, plan my day, and have sex all at the same time."

India laughed. "Please get that picture out of my mind! Besides, aren't those gross generalities about women and men?"

Rhonda shrugged. "All I'm saying is that to create and organize the Universe, you'd have to be able to juggle more than one task at a time. Thus, the Great Mother. But as I said, I don't really know: It's a mystery."

VIOLET WAS ALREADY at the Recreation Center when India and Rhonda walked in. She stood at the back of the gymnasium stretching, her belly bare, her legs in pink tights. Her voluptuous curves undulated to the belly dancing music.

India stopped and stood at the entrance to the gymnasium, watching and wondering how to leave gracefully. Rhonda strode past her into the room. One row of overhead fluorescent lights illuminated Violet and the shiny linoleum floor. The chairs, long tables, and stage were in semi-darkness. Rhonda took off her coat. Beneath she wore a long flowing blue dress with a sheer rose-colored scarf around her waist. She began moving her hips to the music.

"Hello, India. We do stretching exercises first," Violet said.

"Before we shake our sacred booty," Rhonda said.

India rolled her eyes and took off her outer garments. She tied her white shirt below her breasts and pushed her long red skirt down below her navel so that the curve of her waist and belly were exposed. Three more women joined the group: Gina, the postmaster; Ivy who was so skinny India couldn't imagine she had the strength to walk, let alone dance; and Cheryl, a woman from Rhonda's swimming class. Cheryl and Gina were both peripheral members of India's environmental group POOL.

Violet shut off the music and said, "Thank you for signing up again. I don't usually do this in December, but some of you asked me to continue through the holidays. So welcome all. As usual, we need to warm up. Stretch those arms and hands up to the ceiling. Keep your knees relaxed. Breathe."

"All at the same time?" India asked.

Everyone laughed as they reached for the sky, one hand at a time.

"Now the head."

They made circles with their heads, their shoulders, hips.

"Loosen up those hips," Violet said. "That's where the heat comes from."

Rhonda looked at India and winked. India smiled wanly. She did like the feel of her hands on her bare skin as she moved her hips.

After they warmed up their knees and ankles, Violet turned on the music again.

"Feel the beat," Violet said. "Let it flow up through the bottom of your feet. Move to it. Feel your hips start to move on their own."

India closed her eyes for a moment. She had never had problems moving to music; it was structure she couldn't quite get. She did as Violet asked.

Violet taught them how to make figure eights with their hips. India thought she was doing fine until Violet pointed out she was not moving in time to the beat.

"But don't worry about it," Violet said.

"I wasn't until you pointed it out to me," India said.

"Do the best you can." Violet smiled.

India wanted to smack her. How old was Violet? Two? India tried the figure eights again. Why get mad at Violet because she was not particularly graceful? Maybe India was the one who was two.

Violet then showed the group how to drop their hips with "flourish." India watched Violet move her hips as

part of the figure eight with her hands poised elegantly above her head and tried to emulate her.

"With more of a boom," Violet said. "Not a boom. More of a statement. A flourish. Yes, Ivy, that's nice."

How could Violet even tell Ivy was moving?

Finally Violet taught them how to walk while performing the figure eight with a flourish. The six of them snaked around the tables and chairs in time with the music. India's belly and thighs tingled. The music flowed around them, like an ethereal serpent extolling them to dance, to move. India thought they should be outside, dancing naked and howling under a full moon.

Cheryl called, "Yayayayayayaaaa!" Rhonda joined in. Soon all the women were shouting this tribal call to dance.

Jack walked in then. The women danced over to him and surrounded him, shaking their hips and bellies. He blushed and smiled.

Violet was the first to leave the circle. She walked to the cassette player and turned it off.

"Next week, girls," she said.

The group of women stopped dancing and moved away from Jack.

India said to Jack, "I didn't expect to see you."

But she was glad. She was ready to keep dancing. Maybe with him.

"I didn't expect to see you either."

"Oh." So he hadn't seen her car and decided to stop in? He looked away from her. India followed his gaze.

Violet.

"Oh Jack. *Violet*? She's a child."

Jack looked back at her. "Well, I've struck out with women my own age."

India made a noise and went toward Rhonda who was holding India's coat and talking to Cheryl.

Jack put his hand on India's arm. She turned to him. "What?"

"You jealous?" he asked quietly.

"You wish, Jack," she said. "If you get tired of babysitting Violet, come on over."

India turned away and grimaced. She could not believe she had said that. She felt her face reddening. She hurried over to Rhonda and grabbed her coat.

"Get me out of here," she said as she practically ran from the center.

Once outside, Rhonda asked, "What's wrong?"

"I am completely mortified." India unlocked the passenger side of the car for Rhonda, then went around the other side and got in.

"What did you do?"

India started the car. "It's too embarrassing. Let's just say I think I'm having a midlife crisis."

She pulled the car out onto the road. "Did you ever come to a point in your life when you didn't know how you'd gotten to where you were and you couldn't figure out how you could have gotten so many things wrong?"

"Sure, that's called life, honey," Rhonda said.

"I used to be pretty, talented, ambitious. I used to have a future."

"I used to wear a size 9," Rhonda said. "So what?"

"When I was in my twenties I told a friend who was in her late thirties that I was never going to be one of those women who had trouble aging because that was superficial, and I was beyond all that. She must have laughed herself silly. Everything and everyone pisses me off now. Especially other women. Especially younger perky women. I want to slug them. I'm a feminist for goodness sake! Women are my sisters."

India drove the car out onto SR14.

"Women are people, too," Rhonda said. "Some of them piss you off. I've wanted to slug you a few times. You're kind of perky yourself."

"I am not!"

Rhonda laughed. "Listen, kiddo, we're raised from birth to think of other women as competition. Now you've come to that point in your life when you're not the center of the Universe. You're not that prime advertising demographic of twenty to thirty-five year olds. No one is trying to sell you anything. You have to make your own decisions."

"I feel invisible."

"It comes in handy sometimes," Rhonda said. "You can get things done because you're invisible. And because they underestimate you. The important thing is not to become invisible to yourself."

"What does that mean?"

"Have your life," Rhonda said, "on your own terms like you always have. I know you. You don't go for the status quo. Don't start compromising now. Jack used to look at you like he was looking at Violet tonight. You're the one who didn't let it get serious. Remember. He's not your soul mate."

"Soul mate?" India glanced at Rhonda. "Now you're telling me you think we all have soul mates?"

"Yes, we do all have soul mates."

"So who's mine?"

"You've got to figure that out," Rhonda said, "but I wasn't talking about s-o-u-l mate. I meant s-o-l-e mate. We all have a soul mate, and some of us lucky ones have a s-o-l-e mate."

"Which means what?"

"Someone we can walk through life with. A sole mate."

India felt a lump in her throat.

"You know. *Sole. Feet. Walking* through life."

"I get it, Rhonda," India said. "Way to ruin a moment!"

Rhonda laughed. "Take me home, girl. I want to show my sole mate some of the moves we did tonight."

INDIA DANCED AROUND her living room dressed in her panties and a long undershirt. She practiced her figure eights, thinking of them as snakes she created over and over again with her hips. Then she curled up on the couch under her quilt.

She wondered how Benjamin Swan was faring in the cold. And Jack. How was Jack getting along with Violet? If he came over tonight would she let him in? Having sex would not solve all of her problems, but it would be fun. She was comfortable with Jack's little pot belly and the growing bald spot at the top of his head. She knew how to match her rhythm with his, and he always left before he got on her nerves too much.

She sighed. Her relationship with Jack had been her most intimate one in years. She shook her head. She was glad no one but Rhonda knew she and Jack still occasionally hit the sheets together.

At least she assumed no one knew.

She shook herself.

She was cold. She should get up and put on some clothes. But it was cozy here under the quilt. How did Benjamin Swan stay warm? Maybe he had his own version of Violet. She frowned. She could not remember if she had ever made love outside. Too uncomfortable. Too much trouble.

What would it be like to be with a man like Benjamin Swan? First, she supposed, she would have to know what kind of man he was. He looked strong, well-built. None of that really mattered because she could just fall into his gorgeous blue eyes.

She smiled. Next she was going to start wondering what size his penis was. Too big: not good. Too small: not great. Maybe he was just right.

She suddenly felt like Goldilocks in a soft-porn fairy tale.

"Maybe Rhonda was right," India said, closing her eyes. "I need to get laid."

INDIA DREAMED SHE and Benjamin Swan walked along the path near the pond. India looked over her shoulder and saw their footprints in the mud behind them.

She turned to Benjamin and said, "Look, Benjamin Swan, do you know what this means?"

She heard a loud sound, like metal hitting metal, and looked toward the swans. One of them said, "Answer it."

India opened her eyes to darkness. She was standing. That noise. What was that noise? Someone was knocking at the door. She squinted at the clock. 11:00. Had to be Jack.

She rubbed her face.

"Jack?" she called.

Another knock.

Took a lot of nerve for him to go out with one woman and meet another afterward.

Although to be fair, she had stopped at his place after more than one date.

Still. This was not a healthy pattern.

No more knocks.

India looked at the door.

Maybe she should at least talk to him.

She walked across the room.

"Jack?" she said as she swung open the door.

Benjamin Swan stood on her doorstep, holding a backpack.

He glanced at her bare legs, then quickly up to her face.

"Ah, no, Ben," he said.

"I-I don't usually just open the door, especially this late. I thought—"

"I was Jack."

He glanced at her legs again.

"What do you want?" India asked.

"It's snowing and I-I made a mistake. I'm sorry." He turned to go.

"Wait. Come in. Close the door."

She hurried into her bedroom where she put on a pair of slacks and a sweater, then returned to the living room. Benjamin Swan looked uncomfortable. He set the backpack on the floor.

"You got cold?" India said. "Here, take off your coat. Come sit by the heater."

Benjamin unzipped his coat. India reached up and took his hat. It was wet. She looked down at his slacks.

"Are your clothes wet?"

He nodded. He was shivering.

"If I call Jack, he would—"

"He's probably not home," India said. "He had a date tonight. Take off your clothes. I'll put them in the dryer. I don't have any other clothes big enough for you, I don't think." She walked to the bedroom and turned on the light. Benjamin followed her, stopping in the doorway.

"Take off your clothes," she said again.

He pulled off his sweater and began unbuttoning his shirt. India rummaged around the closet until she found an old robe. She held it out to Benjamin.

"Jack's?" he asked.

"I don't really remember," she said.

He started to take off his shirt. He looked almost shell-shocked. And shy. India hesitated. She wanted to see what he looked like shirtless, but she decided that was rude, so she left.

"The laundry room is across the hall."

"Thanks," he said.

India pulled the bedroom door closed. She went into the living room, turned on the lights, and closed the drapes. Then she walked into the kitchen and put water in the kettle and set it on the stove to boil. She took a pot of minestrone from the refrigerator and put it on the stove to warm up.

She leaned against the stove and waited for Benjamin to appear. She heard the dryer start. A few minutes later, Benjamin stepped into the living room. The robe was too small, exposing his muscular legs and arms.

"I feel ridiculous," he said.

"You look fine," India said, crossing her arms across her chest.

"No, I meant for bothering you in the middle of the night when you were expecting—"

"I wasn't expecting anyone," India said. "I was just surprised. Asleep. What happened to you anyway?"

"I'm not sure." He put his hands in the pockets of the robe. "I woke up, and everything was wet."

"You've got your tent set up on the marsh. A *wet*-land."

"Now you tell me."

"I did tell you," India said. "Didn't I? Anyway, I figured you knew what you were doing. The water level must have gone up. It might be raining up river, or they're doing something at the dam. The marsh floods some every winter."

The kettle whistled.

"You want some tea?"

Benjamin shook his head. India frowned. He was still shivering.

"Maybe you should take a shower. You still look cold." She walked over to him and put her hand on his arm. "You're ice cold." She stood in front of him and rubbed his sleeved upper-arms. "Please. Take a shower. I don't want you catching pneumonia. It's an order. Remember what you said about listening to the wisdom of women." She glanced up at him. He watched her. She suddenly realized she was touching him.

She dropped her hands and stepped back.

"Towels are in the linen closet next to the bathroom which is next to the laundry room."

He nodded and left the room.

India waited until she heard the shower turn on. She went to the linen closet and got out bed sheets and carried them to the bedroom. She pulled off the blanket and quilt from the bed and threw them on the chair. Then she pulled off the old sheets and dropped them on the floor. She listened to the water run as she took off the old pillowcases and put on the new. She heard the difference in the flow of the water as Benjamin moved around in the shower. She hoped she hadn't left the bathroom in a mess.

She fitted the corners of the bottom sheet on to the mattress, then put the pillows on the bed. She ran her hands across the pillows, smoothing the wrinkles on the cream-colored cases. She did the same on the sheet, her fingers stopping on a bloodstain. Ah well. She was a woman; she still bled once a month. She refused to use any chemical stain removers that might hurt her or the environment. She could live with an occasional stain. So could Benjamin. She shook the top sheet and let it fall down over the bed. It looked so pretty as it touched the bed, reminding her for a moment of the swan's out-stretched wings waiting for an embrace.

India got the blanket and quilt from the chair and put them over the sheets, then tucked them all in.

She heard the water turn off. She went to the laundry room and checked on Benjamin's clothes. Still wet.

India went to the kitchen and dished out minestrone into her favorite green fiesta ware bowl. She poured hot water into a mug, then carried the bowl, cup, and a spoon to the table.

Benjamin came into the room again. His wet black hair was slicked back against his head. His face was red and shiny.

"My clothes are still wet," he said.

"I know," India said. "You look better. Here, can you eat some soup?"

Benjamin pulled a chair out from the table and sat in it. India sat across from him.

"This is really good," Benjamin said after a couple of spoonfuls. "Fresh vegetables."

"Yes, and all organic." She cleared her throat. "Are you all right? You seem upset."

"I'm OK," he said. "It was strange. I felt like I was a

kid again wetting the bed. When I woke up I didn't know where I was." He glanced around. "I should call Jack."

"No, I changed the sheets on my bed," India said. "You can stay here tonight."

"I didn't know you and Jack were . . . together," he said. This time he did not look at her. He spooned the soup into his mouth.

"We're not," India said. "We had a little fight. I thought maybe he was coming over to smooth things over."

"But that's not all," he said. "Not that it's any of my business."

"Jack and I dated years ago," India said. "Now we're friends."

Benjamin looked at her.

"The best friends are those who have seen you naked," India said. She smiled. "No secrets then."

Benjamin said, "Who wanted out of the relationship?"

"Me."

"I think he's still carrying a torch," Benjamin said. "He does talk about you a lot. I'd heard about you before I ever came out here, but he never said you were seeing one another."

"It's a small town," India said. "We don't know a lot of people, so we tend to talk about those we do know. In a good way, of course." She smiled. "Besides, Jack is dating someone else now."

"You wanted him to come tonight?"

India looked into Benjamin's blue eyes. She hesitated, then said, "I wanted someone to . . . want me."

The silence made India's ears throb.

Benjamin picked up his dishes and took them to the sink.

"I'll do those in the morning," she said.

"I really don't want to take your bed," Benjamin said. "I can sleep on the couch."

"Naked?" India said. "I don't think our friendship has progressed that far yet."

Benjamin smiled. "Yet?" He looked like himself again—only dressed in some short man's old robe.

India went to him and put her hand on his back. They walked to the bedroom.

"Have a good sleep," India said.

Benjamin turned to her and took her left hand in his. He brought it up to his mouth, turned it over, and gently kissed her palm.

"Thank you," he said.

"Sure," was all she managed to say as she took her hand back.

She went into the bedroom, turned on the bedside lamp, and picked up her pillow.

"See you in the morning," she said.

She turned her back on him and walked away. Before she reached the living room, she heard her name. She tossed the pillow on the couch and went back to the bedroom. Benjamin Swan lay in her bed, covered by her blankets, except for his shoulders and arms. And part of his chest. She sighed. She *must* be going through a midlife crisis. She wanted to crawl into bed with this man. This man who did not appear to have a single gray

Kim Antieau

hair on him.

"Yes?" she said.

"You want to know what I was grinning at today, out in the meadow, when you thought I was making fun of you?"

"OK. What were you grinning at?"

"I was suddenly so happy walking with you, listening to your stories, watching you stand there on the path, gesturing as you talked about your days as a rebel girl scout. You looked so beautiful."

India's breath caught in her throat. She did not know what to say. She was not beautiful. How could he say something like that to her? Was he trying to placate the nice old lady because she had told him about Jack? About wanting to be wanted.

Tears sprung to her eyes. She turned away. She would not let him see he had hurt her.

She grabbed for the doorknob.

"Good night," she said as she closed the door.

She angrily wiped the tears away as she went into the living room. She switched off the lights, then stretched out on the couch. She closed her eyes.

"I was suddenly happy walking next to you. . . . You looked so beautiful." India shook her head, trying to shake away Benjamin Swan's blue eyes. He had not been trying to be cruel. She could see that in the memory of his eyes. He had meant what he said.

No. That couldn't be. She looked at herself every morning. She saw what he saw.

Maybe not.

Maybe he meant a different kind of beauty.

Maybe he meant beautiful in a different way than beautiful.

He could not have meant she was beautiful in a beautiful sexy way.

He must have been saying she was beautiful, like an old hippie saying, You're beautiful, man.

Yes. That was it.

He was not being cruel. He was not saying he wanted her.

Even though he had seemed upset that she was expecting Jack. Relieved when she said they were no longer together.

It was not possible that a man like Benjamin Swan— a man who looked like him—could want a woman like her.

She opened her eyes and stared into the darkness. She held up her hand but could not see it.

Had she become invisible to herself?

She sighed.

"Go to sleep," she whispered.

CHAPTER FIVE

INDIA OPENED HER eyes and saw Benjamin Swan sitting at the kitchen table looking at his hands. He was dressed in a T-shirt and jeans. India ran her hand through her hair as she sat up. Benjamin turned to her.

"Good morning," he said. "I hope the couch was comfortable."

"I can sleep anywhere," India said, yawning.

"Except outside in a tent," Benjamin said.

"Yes, except there," India said. "How are you?"

"Better," he answered.

India got up and opened the curtains. Gray clouds covered the sky. Snow dusted the ground. Swans bobbed on the pond in the distance.

"I think I was almost sleepwalking or in shock or

something last night," Benjamin said. "That's got to be the only explanation."

India looked at him. "Explanation for what?"

"For me telling you I wet the bed when I was a boy," he said. "Now that's the only thing you know about me. What an image!"

India laughed.

"Shall I make my rescuer some breakfast?" Benjamin asked. He stretched and yawned. He looked good in jeans and a T-shirt.

"OK," India said.

"What do you want?"

"Scrambled tofu."

Benjamin went into the kitchen. India sat on a stool at the counter. He opened the refrigerator and took out a package of tofu.

"You know what tofu looks like," India said. "I'm impressed. I took you for a meat and potatoes kind of guy."

Benjamin held the package out to her. "It says tofu right on the label."

India laughed. "OK. This is what you do: Saute a little bit of onion. Don't let it get too hot or burn it because then the whole dish is bitter. Drain the tofu, then crumble it into the pan. Add about two teaspoons of tamari, one teaspoon of curry, a half teaspoon of turmeric, and a bit of sage. Then cook it until it's hot. Bread is in the freezer. You can figure out the rest. I'm taking a shower."

"I can handle it," he said. "Onions are these long orange things, right?"

India smiled, then went to the bathroom. She closed the door, took off her clothes, and glanced in the mirror.

"Gawd," she said.

She leaned into the shower and turned on the water. No hair in the drain, no towels on the floor. Benjamin was gorgeous and neat.

She smiled, stepped into the shower, and let the hot water pour over her. She sighed with pleasure. As she looked down at her body, she ran her hand over her breasts and along her side where her waist curved in and then out to become her hip. She cupped her rounded belly with both hands. Her Renaissance belly, she had always called it. She made figure eights with her hips. Belly dancing in the shower. She laughed and reached for the shampoo.

When India returned to the living room/kitchen/dining room, the wooden table was set with two plates—one apricot, one green—and two cups and silverware. Benjamin stood over the plates spooning the golden scrambled tofu onto them, next to slices of apple.

India pulled out a chair and sat at the green plate. Benjamin returned the pan to the stove, picked up a plate of toast, then brought it to the table. He set the toast down as he sat next to India. He rested his arm inches from hers. She picked up her fork and began eating.

"Good job," she said.

"Just followed directions." He ate a few bites. "This isn't bad."

"What have you been eating these past couple of weeks?" India asked.

"Camping rations mostly. Plus Jack and I have gone out a couple of times."

"Why don't you go live with Jack?" India said. "It's only a couple of miles down the road."

"I want to be near the swans," he said. "I want to wake up to their sounds, watch them fly, rest, eat."

India took a bite of toast and nodded.

"You can't stay on the marsh," India said.

"If I get too close to the swans, they fly away," Benjamin said.

"I love the swans, too," India said, "but I'm satisfied to watch them from here on really cold days."

"When I was a kid my mother used to tell me swan stories," Benjamin said. "She talked about the Knight of Swans who was around during King Arthur's time and before. His duty was to help those women who were having trouble adjusting to patriarchal times. Only my mom didn't say patriarchal. She didn't know that word then. She said those women who had trouble fitting into a man's world. They had once had power and no longer did, and the Swan Knight was responsible for them. To help them make the adjustment."

"You mean to assimilate them?"

"To help them in whatever way they needed," Benjamin said. "She also told me stories of the Swan Maidens. Have you heard of them?"

"I think I have, but tell me anyway." She bit into an apple slice.

"They were swans who shapechanged into women or women who shapechanged into swans," Benjamin said.

"They flew down to Earth from their place in the up-perworld—or underworld—and danced at the edges of lakes, throwing off their magical cloaks of swan feathers which made them into swans. If a man stole one of those cloaks, the Swan Maiden was obligated to become his bride. But if she ever found the cloak again, she would throw it over her shoulders as she ran outside into the wild, becoming a swan as she went, her arms stretch-ing into wings, her vertebrae curving into a swan's neck. She would not hesitate once she had the cloak again; she would leave everything behind: husband, home, children. Well, those stories were told to me when I was a boy looking into my mother's sad eyes. If I were the Swan Knight, I knew my job was to find my mother's feather cloak. That was how I could help her. But I never found it." He glanced out the window, then looked at India. "I guess one of the reasons I wanted to be here and study the swans was to see if I could figure out from them how to be in this world—how to find my place in it."

They finished eating in silence.

"Get your coat," India said. "I just remembered some-thing."

India pushed her hat down on her still wet hair, put on her jacket, slipped on her shoes, and grabbed her keys. They stepped out into an icy wind. India ran to the de-tached garage, then up the stairs that went alongside it. She unlocked the door and went inside to a room above the garage about the size of her living room. Benjamin stepped in behind her and shut the door.

"I had forgotten all about this," she said, walking

around the clutter to stand in front of a picture window that looked out at the pond and swans. "My landlord had this made for their teenaged son who wanted his own room. It's heated, has a bathroom and sink but no shower. The view is the same as the one out my living room, only better because it's higher up. I use it for storage, but you could move my stuff to one side or put it in the garage. Clean this place up a bit, get a hot plate, turn on the heat, and you're laughing."

"Are you saying I can stay here?"

India laughed. "It's not a tent, but it's pretty rough."

Benjamin looked around. She smiled. Her heart was racing. She knew now she had lost her mind. She was inviting a complete stranger to live with her.

"You can use my shower as long as it wasn't every day," India said, "and pay the difference in my heat and water bills." She shrugged. "My way of helping save the swans. Look." She slid the window open. "Probably if you listened really hard you could hear the swans from here, too."

Benjamin looked at her. "I guess this means I didn't completely scare you last night. Or else you feel sorry for me."

"I'm hoping you'll keep cooking for me."

"It's a deal," Benjamin said. "I'll take it. Thank you."

India pulled the key off her ring. "This opens the garage and this door."

Benjamin took the key from her.

"Don't worry," India said. "I won't invade your privacy. We don't even have to see each other."

Benjamin frowned. "I want to see you."

Silence again. India looked away from him.

Benjamin said, "I better get my stuff on the marsh. I had enough sense to bring my notes and camera with me last night, but I'm not sure about the rest."

"I would offer to help, but it's too freaking cold," India said. "You can borrow my vacuum cleaner if you need it and use the washer and dryer if your clothes got wet." She looked at him. "I don't know why I'm doing this. I'm usually very territorial. I don't like people in my stuff."

"Like swans," Benjamin said. "They've been known to break a man's leg when he got too close to a nest."

"I won't break your leg," India said, "but I may change my mind or get really cranky, and you'll wish I would just break your leg and get it over with. It's freezing. I'm going back to the house."

"Thanks again, India Lake."

India ran down the steps and into the house. She leaned against the closed door to catch her breath. She sighed deeply and grinned. It was kind of fun going crazy.

The phone rang. India picked it up.

"Good morning, India," Jack said.

"Hello."

"Did you miss me last night?" he asked.

India sighed. "What do you want?"

Jack cleared his throat. "I want to let you know there's going to be a public meeting next week about the Dutch property."

"The Dutch property?" That was the official name of Turtle Pond and environs. India's stomach lurched. "Why? What's happening?"

"We've had an offer to trade the Dutch land for two hundred acres of pristine wilderness up near Indian Heaven."

"Trade with whom?"

"First," Jack said, "let me tell you I've done some investigating. It's really going to be all right."

"Jack."

"Aviary Lumber. But they have promised to protect the pond and the rest of the property," he said quickly. "They initiated this transfer as a kind of charity. They're known for their conservation practices. There's no trees to cut down on the property, really. They can't do anything else because of the National Scenic Act. And we've wanted the land near Indian Heaven forever. It's got old growth."

"I don't understand then," India said. "Why don't they just give you the Indian Heaven land if they want this to be a charitable act. Why the trade?"

"Apparently it's better for their corporate tax situation," Jack said. "Plus, the commissioners really want the Dutch property back as part of the county. Then they can collect taxes on it."

India stared out at the pond as they talked. Eighty-five percent of the land in Shahalla County was owned by some government entity, so the county coffers were always starved for cash.

"They won't get much tax money on a strip of land

that by their definition isn't producing anything," India said.

"It'll be something," Jack said. "And get this, India. They said they want the cattle gone."

"Wow," India said. She sat on the couch and felt the knot in her stomach start to unwind. "So this could be good news."

"Could be," Jack said.

They were silent for a moment.

"Do you want me to come over tonight?" Jack asked.

India hesitated, then said, "No, I've got a POOL meeting this afternoon, and I'm not sure I'll feel like seeing another human being ever again after that."

Jack laughed. India smiled. She had always liked his laugh. She could never stay mad at him for long.

"Thanks for calling, Jack," India said. "I trust your judgment on this matter. I usually trust you. Well, most of the time."

"Talk about a backhanded compliment," he said. "There's my other line. I need to get it. See you later."

"Bye, Jack."

"Good bye, love."

India hung up and stared at the phone. "Bye, *love*?" she said out loud. She and Jack had never been mushy with each other, had never been in love—at least not with each other.

He must have been joking.

AFTER INDIA HAD her lunch, members of POOL began arriving. Rhonda and Beth came together; Marian and

Nancy arrived separately. They all sat around the kitchen table discussing strategy while eating sandwiches they had brought. India sat quietly and listened. She had learned not to expect much from these meetings. POOL stood for Pesticides Out of Our Lives, and they tried to convince the county to (at least) reduce roadside spraying and get the schools to completely eliminate pesticide use. So far POOL had not even succeeded in getting the county to admit that children should not be exposed to pesticides. The entire group had been on a committee to try and create an Integrated Vegetation and Pest Management plan for the county. It was POOL versus the good ol' boys. Every time the women made a suggestion the Washington State extension agent countered with, "Where is the scientific proof these pesticides are harmful?" And when they brought him proof, he would say, "That isn't proof. This group has an agenda."

"Yes, unlike the agenda-less pesticide companies who deny their chemicals could hurt anything!" India would roar. "I'm surprised they admit pesticides actually kill bugs and weeds. Our *agenda* is public safety. Their agenda is to make money!"

For India, the meetings brought out the true meaning of the acronym POOL: Pissed Off Old Ladies.

"We need to keep going after the county before they start spraying this spring," Marian said now, chewing her sandwich with an open mouth.

"They have to comply with the new federal rules to protect the salmon," Beth said. "We must make certain they adhere—"

Kim Antieau

"What exactly is the language of those rules?" Nancy asked.

Beth glared at her. "If you'd let me finish."

"I don't want to get bogged down in that," Marian said.

"If they have to save the salmon, they have to stop spraying," Beth said. "If you would read the regulations. I e-mailed them to you all."

"I wish we were more organized," Marian said.

"We don't need any more organization," Nancy said. "You need to go to the commissioners' meetings and get them to change their policies."

"The commissioners are assholes," India said.

"Well, they got voted out," Rhonda said.

"And new assholes take their place," India said. "Look, I've tried working with the commissioners for four years. I used to think most people are trying to do a good job and just get through the day, but this whole thing with the county and what I see as their mismanagement of pesticides has changed my mind. They're good ol' boys and girls trying to protect their own backsides, and that's it. I'm tired of trying to work through a system that ain't working."

"A friend of mine who used to be on the planning board here said that after many frustrating years she started waiting it out, you know, hoping they'd all get old and die out," Rhonda said, "but then she realized they were multiplying and their offspring had their same values."

"I don't like coming from such a place of negativity,"

Marian said. "I want to go toward something positive."

"A class action suit," India said. "That would be positive."

"I've been talking to Daniel Salmonson about the lawsuit, as POOL requested," Beth said. "In fact, he's going to be in town tomorrow and I'm having lunch with him at the Crossroads at 1:00. You're all welcome to join us. He's going to let us know what he thinks about a class action suit."

"I'll try to be there," India said.

"We should concentrate on the schools," Nancy said. "Write letters to the paper. I don't think most parents or teachers realize their schools are regularly sprayed with pesticides, inside and out."

"No one reads the paper," India said. "No one cares."

The women looked at her.

"I'm sorry," India said. "I'm tired of dealing with these people. I can't get them to see Nature as important. I can't make them feel as passionately about this place as I do. And it makes me weep. It makes me want to give up. So I get angry, righteously angry. We need that anger sometimes to help us go forward." She looked out the window. In reality, she had not felt like going forward, backward, or anywhere for a long while. She wanted to be some place where things were easy.

"Talk to the superintendent of the schools," Nancy said. "Go to the power sources."

"Speaking of power sources," India said. "Jack called today. The state is considering exchanging the Dutch property for two hundred acres in Indian Heaven now owned by Aviary Lumber."

The woman all stopped and stared at India.

Finally Marian said, "That's terrible. I know how much you love this place."

"I think it'll be OK," India said. "Jack says they aren't going to develop the property. In fact, they can't. And they're going to kick out the cattle."

Beth shook her head. "Something fishy about this."

"I was shocked, too," India said, "until Jack said he'd investigated and was satisfied it's all above board."

"You place too much faith in Jack," Nancy said. "He's the one who let the cattle come in the first place."

"And you know I fought that all the way," India said. "And that stupid barbed wire. I think we should investigate this and attend the meeting. That's why I brought it up."

India heard a knock. She got up from the table and went to the door and opened it. Benjamin stood in the doorway holding a bag of what India took to be clothes.

"They're soaked," Benjamin said.

"You know the way to the laundry," India said, waving him in.

"Thanks." He smiled at her. It seemed as though he positively glowed. India smiled. How wonderful to be so joyous.

"Hi, ladies," he said.

"Hello, Benjamin," Rhonda said.

"Benjamin, these are my friends Marian, Nancy, Beth. We're all part of this environmental group. We're trying to bring down the man."

"Any particular man?" Benjamin asked.

"*The* man," India said.

"Good luck to you."

India watched Benjamin walk away.

Then she looked at the silent women.

"What?" she said. She sat with them again. "Are we going to decide on a plan of action about the roadside spraying or what?"

"We've got to move forward," Marian said, "positively."

"The commissioners are the ones with the power," Nancy said.

"Maybe the schools," Rhonda said.

India rolled her eyes. It was a wonder they ever accomplished anything. Five very independent women made up the core of the group and they all had their own ideas. India had hoped to foster a sense of community originally when forming the group with Beth, but none of them seemed to know how to work as a team. India refused to lead them—not that it would have done any good anyway. They were all leaders. Not a follower among them. Of course, none of the rest of the members were troubled by the direction the group was taking—whatever direction that was. Only India. Maybe something was wrong with her. Now that she thought about it, she was the baby of the group; Beth was the oldest. The dozen or more women involved in POOL ranged in ages from 45 to about 75, in varying stages of pissed off and old lady.

Benjamin came into the room again.

"Do you want me to stay and watch the clothes?" Benjamin asked.

The women turned to look at India.

"No, I'll put them in the dryer," India said.

The women turned their heads to Benjamin.

"You want me to make dinner?" Benjamin asked. He was grinning and had a twinkle in his eye. He knew he was performing for the women. India smiled.

"Or we can have soup again," India said.

"See you later then. Oh, and I will borrow the vacuum."

"In the closet next to the door," India said.

The women watched Benjamin open the door and bend over to pick up the vacuum. India snapped her fingers.

"Hey, we've got some work to do," she said.

When Benjamin left, the women busily flipped through their folders.

"He's studying the swans," India said. "I'm letting him use the room over the garage."

"He stayed at my house, too," Rhonda said. "He's a nice man."

"So you're letting him stay here all for the cause?" Nancy asked.

"I'm not sure why I offered," India said. "Maybe I wanted the company."

Rhonda raised her eyebrows.

"What?" India asked.

"You're so private," Marian said. "We'd follow you anywhere, but you always put a time limit on every visit.

Now you're going to have a stranger underfoot all of the time."

"Sometimes strangers are easier," Rhonda said. "No expectations."

"That's true," Beth said. "I prefer my time alone." She glanced over at India. "Is this because you think Jack is dating Violet?"

India looked at Rhonda.

"I didn't tell her," Rhonda said.

"Jack?" Marian asked. "Jack Combs? You haven't dated him in years."

"No, but she still sleeps with him," Nancy said.

"What!" India said.

"It's not a secret," Nancy said.

"Well, I thought it was," India said. "I mean I don't talk about my sex life with anyone."

"And more's the pity," Rhonda said. "Isaac says he admires women because we can so easily talk about intimate things. But you know, as a rule, we don't really talk specifically about our sex lives."

"You mean like the part about her not wanting it when I do," Nancy said.

"Or him wanting it all of the time," Marian said. "That's why I gave up on men. They're too much trouble."

"Women aren't any easier," Nancy said.

"A friend of mine once took me to a woman's commune in Estacada, I think," Beth said. "They all had their tops off. Their breasts hanging out in the sun. I was really annoyed because she hadn't told me what kind of place it was."

India laughed. "What kind of place do you mean, Beth? I've been there. They do the We'Moon calendar date book every year. I went one August for a harvest celebration. It was wonderful. You could immediately tell who was a lesbian and who was a hetero. All the straight women kept their tops on. I was kind of in-between. No bra, but I left on my camisole. I loved being there. I felt so safe and free. Not like I actually fit in, but like I was closer to being the real me. There was something wild about being out in the woods with bare naked women. When I left that afternoon, I remember driving off the land and putting on my shirt and locking my car door. I had to be on guard again. I drove away crying. I've never been back. The contrast between that world where Nature and women mattered to this one was just too stark."

"I never went back either," Beth said. "Too many bare breasts."

They all laughed.

"But back to sex," Rhonda said.

India laughed. "Sex is too hard to talk about because we all think our sex life is weird and everyone else's is just like in the movies or in books."

"That's right," Nancy said. "Like in your book. Your characters have great cosmic sex. It raises unrealistic expectations."

"If you're going to have sex, why bother unless it is cosmic?" India asked.

"No, really. Your characters get on, get off, then get

off," Nancy said. "It's not realistic."

"Maybe not to you," India said.

"OK," Beth said. "That's enough for me. I need to get going. We'll see you later."

Rhonda helped Beth find her coat. They called good-bye to her as she left.

"What's so great about realism anyway?" India asked. "For one thing, my main character had gone through terrible trials and tribulations. When she finally found a lover I wasn't going to have them have bad sex. Come on! I write a lot about food, too, but I usually don't describe the sound of chewing or the pieces of food stuck in someone's teeth—not if I'm trying to be sensual. Same with sex. I don't talk about the wet spot or how long it took to insert penis into vagina, or whatever kind of genitalia goes with another kind of genitalia."

"That's what I mean," Nancy said. "Aren't all of those things part of the experience?"

"But that's not sexy," Rhonda said.

"When you're first with someone," Marian said, "you don't really notice those things. You're lost in passion."

"That passes," Nancy said. "We need stories about sexual passion after you've seen the other person throwing up, shitting, burping, in the morning with snot on their face. We need stories about what comes after they live happily ever after."

"See, we're still not really talking about sex," Rhonda said.

"OK," India said. "You first. What sexual secret do you have to share?"

"You mean something I don't want people to know about?" Rhonda asked.

"Not too much detail," Marian said. "We have to see each other again after tonight."

"Who was your strangest lover?" Nancy asked.

"This old Marxist I dated in college," Rhonda said. "He wouldn't have intercourse. He was afraid I'd get pregnant, he said. So we had to satisfy each other in different ways, and he took forever. I got repetitive stress syndrome before they had a name for it."

India and Nancy laughed. Marian moaned.

"Mine was with this guy with a huge penis," Nancy said.

"A man?" Marian said. "I didn't know you did that."

"When I was young and foolish," Nancy said. "He was so proud of it. It was really wide and difficult to get in, so to speak. He talked about it as though it was separate from him."

"Yeah, I hate it when they name it," Marian said, "like we're supposed to bow down to it."

They all laughed.

"I haven't had sex in years," Marian said. "I can't really remember what it was like."

"Your turn, India."

"I've had some strange experiences," India said, "I guess. My first sexual encounters were with a boy I went to high school with. It was great. We learned how to do it on each other's bodies. I could tell when he started having sex with other women. He moved differently. It was never the same. Then I had a guy who was quick on the trigger. Really quick. I had a couple who wouldn't have intercourse either, Rhonda, so maybe it isn't that strange. One guy had a teeny tiny penis. I touched it in the dark and had to bite my tongue to keep from screaming—I thought there was something wrong with it. I think I figured out later it was flaccid. I was used to being around all of these boys with constant hard-ons." The women laughed. "Dated a poet who wrote the most sensuous, sexy poems. But he was a terrible lover. Didn't have the meat or the motion. And he was really, really white. Then there was Raymond. I don't know what happened. I thought we were happy, but then it seemed he didn't like me anymore. He didn't satisfy me in any way. After a while his penis would not go into my vagina. Strangest thing. It was like I put up some kind of wall or checkpoint Charlie at my vagina. You may not enter. Worried me a lot, but I didn't do anything to fix it. He stopped trying after a while. Eventually found himself another babe."

"He was your husband?" Marian asked.

"No, I never married," India said. "But we were together for a long time."

"Was she younger?" Rhonda asked.

"The babe? Sure. Then there was Jack. He was great because his penis fit into my vagina."

They all laughed.

"That's a plus," Rhonda said.

"I was back in working order," India said. "But I never loved him, so we became friends."

"And you're still sleeping together?" Marian asked.

"Apparently not anymore," India said.

"Wow, when you spill your guts, you really go, girl," Nancy said.

India's face flushed. This was why she did not like to get personal: She never knew what she was supposed to say or keep to herself.

"Really there's too much fuss about sex and compatibility," Rhonda said. "If you're going to be with someone, find someone who makes you laugh."

"And rings your bell," Marian said.

They began putting their trash into the paper sacks they had brought. India picked up the cups and spoons.

"This Benjamin guy looks like he could ring someone's bell real good," Nancy said.

"Good grief," India said.

"So you haven't noticed his blue eyes or gorgeous ass?" she asked.

"Are you sure you're a lesbian?" Rhonda asked.

Nancy laughed. "Are you sure you're not?"

"We probably are all lesbians," Marian said. "We've been brainwashed to believe men will rescue us. That's bullshit. We do the heavy lifting. We raise the kids, bury the dead, take care of the sick and grieving, try to fix the messes."

"You go, sister!" India said.

"We're the ones who will save the world!" Rhonda called out, Baptist preacher-like as she carried her trash to the garbage under the sink.

"Hallelujah!" India said.

"Some of them do look mighty fine in a tight pair of

jeans," Marian said.

"Careful girl," Nancy said. "You're drooling."

CHAPTER SIX

INDIA CLEANED THE house after the women left. She had not been out all day. The cold dreary day had made her want to cocoon, or put her head under her wing like the swans did.

She heated up the soup, then took out red and green leafed lettuce and ripped it into bits. She grated a carrot over it. A spot of olive oil. Perfect. Everything was set for her dinner with Benjamin.

When she heard a knock on her door, she called, "Come in."

"I could have been the Boston strangler. Since when do you leave the door unlocked?"

India turned around.

Jack. Not Benjamin.

What, was her life suddenly becoming an English farce?

Jack glanced over at the set kitchen table, then at the steaming soup, and chilled salad.

"Ahhh," he said. "You were expecting someone else."

"Just Benjamin," India said, trying to sound casual. "You're welcome to stay, too."

But don't, she pleaded silently.

"If you're sure I'm not intruding," he said.

India took a plate and bowl from the cupboard and handed them to Jack. "Go set yourself a place. What are you doing here anyway? I told you I didn't want company."

"But apparently you did. I just wasn't the right company."

India shook her head and tossed the salad. Out of the corner of her eye, she saw Jack stop at the table and look at the place settings. They were next to one another instead of across the table: more intimate than he expected, she supposed. He paused, hesitated, then put his dinner ware across from the blue plate and next to the green one. He knew her favorite was the green.

India shook her head. Like a dog marking his territory.

"How was your date with Violet?" India asked. She handed him the salad bowl as he turned to her. He set it on the table.

"Fine," he said. "She's a nice kid."

"Good," India said.

"Benjamin's truck is fixed," Jack said. "I'll have to remember to tell him."

India nodded.

A knock at the door.

India went to it and asked who it was.

"Ben."

She opened the door. Benjamin Swan stood there covered from head to foot with dust, dirt, and spider webs.

"I tried to wash it all off in the sink," Benjamin said.

"Go," India said, pointing toward the bathroom. "Your clean clothes are in the dryer. You know where the towels are."

Benjamin took off his shoes. "Hello, Jack."

"Benjamin."

India went to the kitchen as Benjamin headed for the bathroom. She kept her back to Jack and tried to find something to busy her hands with. She stirred the soup.

Jack finally said, "You're doing his *laundry*?"

"No! The marsh came up last night. Everything got wet so I let him use the washing machine. I'm letting him stay in the room over the garage, too."

"He's living here?" Jack said.

India heard the shower come on.

"He's not living *here*," she said. "He's your friend." She turned to face Jack. "He's here to learn about the swans. I care about Turtle Pond and the swans. I'm trying to help out. Why are you giving me attitude?"

"First, you know nothing about him," Jack said.

"He's your friend. You said he's a good guy."

"He is," Jack said, "but he's had some hard times. I

wouldn't want—"

"Wouldn't want what?" India interrupted.

Jack stared at her.

"Why are we fighting?" India asked.

"You started it yesterday," he said.

India laughed. "God, you are obnoxious." She threw an apple at him. He caught it before it hit his face.

"Hey!" Jack got off the stool and came around the counter. "Two can play this game."

India laughed as he caught her around the waist. He put the apple up to her mouth. She tried to take a bite. Jack pulled it away—and leaned down and kissed her mouth.

Then he whispered, "I drove here last night after my date. I sat in the car trying to decide if I should come in or not."

India pulled away. "Jack," she said.

He reached for her.

Benjamin came into the living room. India quickly stepped away from Jack.

"Hey, old man," Jack said. "Hope you don't mind if I join you for supper."

Benjamin glanced at India.

"It's India's house."

"Let's eat," India said. "This is going to turn to mush. Jack, put that trivet on the table. Benjamin, sit."

India carried the pot to the table.

Jack sat at the apricot-colored plate. Benjamin started to sit across from him, but India said, "Here, there's more room for you. You two buddies can sit beside each

Kim Antieau

other and catch up."

Benjamin shrugged and took his place. India sat next to him.

"Jack, will you serve the soup?"

He nodded, then filled their bowls, one at a time, starting with India.

"Oh, I forgot, I was heating up some bread in the oven," India said.

"I'll get it," both men started to rise.

"Sit down," India said. She went to the oven, slid the bread out and dropped it onto the plate, then returned with it to the table.

"India says you're moving into the garage," Jack said.

"Yeah, I didn't get to spend much time with the swans today," Benjamin said. "My stuff got a little flooded last night. You should come up and see the room, India. It looks nice. A little dusty was all."

She smiled and kept eating. This was not how she had seen the evening progressing.

She buttered the warm bread and took a bite.

What had she hoped would happen tonight?

Benjamin could have come into the house as she got out of the shower. Their gazes would lock. He would be overcome with desire and have to have her right then and there.

"With your permission, my lady," he would say before unbuttoning his orange parka and laying bare his—

"India? India? Hello!" Jack's voice.

"Hmm. What?"

"Do you know if the room over the garage is up to code?" Jack asked.

"I assume so. My landlord's son lived there."

"I wouldn't want you to get into trouble," Jack said.

"Don't be a fussbudget," India said. "Everything will be fine."

Jack opened his mouth, then shut it again. His bald spot reddened. India tried to think of something to say.

"It's sweet of you, Jack, really. But it'll be fine. How did you two meet anyway?"

"We went to college together," Benjamin said.

"You two are the same age?" India asked.

"I'm a few years older," Jack said. "I started school later. We were roommates for a while, but Benjamin was too wild for me."

Benjamin shook his head. "Not true."

"Women flocked to him," Jack said. "I couldn't keep up."

"That was a long time ago," Benjamin said.

"He probably had every woman on campus at one time or another," Jack said.

Benjamin looked at his friend.

"So what'd you go to college for?" India asked.

"Teaching," Jack answered. "Ben is a teacher. Or *was* a teacher. Isn't that right, Benji? Had a little trouble, didn't you? Did he tell you about that?"

Benjamin stared into his soup.

"Jack, we're having a conversation," India said, "not revealing state secrets. Benjamin, how's the soup?"

Benjamin looked at her. "Still good." He picked up

his spoon and continued eating.

India gave Jack a look.

"Anyway, we've been friends for a long time," Jack said.

"What did you and Violet do last night?" India asked, changing the subject.

"We went out to dinner," Jack said.

"Did she teach you some belly dancing moves?" India asked.

"A few," Jack said. This time, he gave her a look. She smiled and stared at him. She wanted to kick him under the table, but she was afraid she would kick Benjamin instead.

They finished their meal in silence.

"Can I do the dishes?" Benjamin asked.

India shook her head. "Let Jack."

Jack leaned back in his chair and looked around the room. Then he glanced at Benjamin.

"Have you shown India any of your drawings or photos?" Jack asked, his tone conciliatory.

Benjamin shook his head. "I haven't put them on my computer yet.

"He's really an artist," Jack said.

Benjamin shifted uncomfortably in his seat.

Jack looked around the room again.

"I'll go get my clothes," Benjamin said.

"You can fold them right there," India said. "If you want."

Benjamin got up and left the room.

"I thought you two were friends," India said as she

and Jack began clearing the table. "Why are you trying to make him uncomfortable?"

"I was trying to put him at ease."

"You were acting like a bully," India said. "I don't like you very much right now. I want you to go home."

They put the dishes in the sink.

"I'm sorry," Jack said. "I felt like I was in college again—the third wheel—while Benjamin got the girl."

"No one is getting any girl," India said. "Except perhaps you because you're dating one."

"I'll call you later."

Jack left the house and walked into the cold night alone.

India put her hands on each side of the sink and sighed. After a moment, she turned around. Benjamin stood in the living room.

"I didn't want to scare you," Benjamin said.

"I'm sorry about Jack," India said. "He can be such an asshole."

"I don't really understand what's going on here," Benjamin said. "I don't want to get in the middle of anything."

India shook her head. "I don't really know what's going on either. With Jack. Is that what you meant?"

"I think he's still in love with you," Benjamin said.

India shook her head. "No. He's probably nervous about Violet, so he came here for someone familiar."

"I'm sorry," Benjamin said. "This is personal between you and Jack. It's none of my business." He looked at her. "He's being protective of you. All that stuff about women. I had lots of women friends. I wasn't sleeping with them. That's not me."

India watched him. He looked so big, strong, and able to take care of himself, yet there was something tender-hearted about him, too. Breakable.

"Benjamin—"

"He wanted you to know about me," Benjamin said. "I was a teacher. There was this girl."

"Oh." India felt all the wind go out of her.

Benjamin tried to hold her gaze. "That's why I didn't want to tell you. People hear that one line, and they've tried and convicted me. I taught art, photography, and history. I was a good teacher. I really cared about the students. I was there because I wanted to be there. Over in Mott, Oregon. This girl, Melanie, was pretty troubled. I tried to help her out. She was having such a difficult time being in the world. Her parents were drunks and didn't know anything about her life. But I was never alone with her. I'm not stupid."

India leaned against the sink.

"One day out of the blue, I was called to the principal's office. My union rep is there, and I'm told I'm suspended. No hearing, no trial. They show me a photograph of Melanie, naked, sitting on a chair in my classroom. She says I took the picture and then had sexual relations with her. India, the police raided my house. Tore everything apart. After a few hours they finally found what they wanted: a naked picture of my niece when she was two playing the drums. They took me down to the police station and accused me of being a child pornographer and a child molester. I called my lawyer. They never pressed any charges but the accusation was there. At first people came to my defense, but then it was discovered she was pregnant, and she insisted I was the father. I was vilified in the papers. People stopped speaking to me. I thought the truth will out. But it didn't. I insisted on a paternity test. Finally, after three months, she admitted she'd made the whole thing up. She was so messed up that she believed her parents wouldn't mind if she was pregnant by a teacher, because I had a job and an education, instead of her low-life drug-addicted boyfriend. It turned out he had taken the nude photos, too."

Benjamin stopped. He looked at the floor.

"I never did anything wrong." He looked up at her again. "Ever. But my reputation was destroyed anyway. They took me off suspension because they had to. By then it was nearly summer. And I couldn't go back this fall. I wished I could have, but I was so hurt and angry. Tainted. Everything feels tainted."

"I'm sorry that happened to you," she said. "I can't even imagine what that would be like."

"Jack was trying to protect you from the taint of being associated with an accused child molester and pornographer. I'm sorry. I should have told you before I took the room."

"The room? I don't care about this. You tried to help someone. I know it. You were trying to be the Swan Knight. You thought you were helping her find her magical cloak, but she turned on you."

"So did everyone else," Benjamin said. "Except my

family and Jack. He never doubted me. Or didn't seem to until tonight."

"Oh, Benjamin, tonight was Jack trying to piss further than the next guy—which happened to be you. Please don't let tonight affect your friendship."

"I'm a little tired," he said. "I think I'll call it a night. Thank you for dinner. And for the room."

India nodded. She wished she knew what to say or do to make him feel better.

"I'll see you tomorrow," she said.

He went to the door, got his coat, and put it on.

"Good night," he said.

The room pulsed with silence after he left. India telephoned Jack. The machine picked up.

"Jack," she said when the message finished, "you better come see Benjamin tomorrow. He told me what happened at his school, and now he's worried you doubt him." She paused. "Do the right thing, Jack. I've got nothing to do with your relationship with Benjamin. Be his friend."

She hung up the phone, turned off the lights, and went to her bedroom.

"So much for my fantasy life," she said as she got into her cold bed.

CHAPTER SEVEN

THE SUN CAME out the next morning, its light turning to silver gold as it streamed through wispy clouds, causing steam to rise from the pond and ground like some conjuror's trick.

India stood at the window with a cup of hot water between her hands. She spotted Benjamin's orange parka on the river side of the cottonwood. And a green fish and wildlife coat. Jack.

Good.

Now she could stop thinking about them and figure out what she was going to do with her time.

She waited until Benjamin and Jack were no longer in sight. Then she bundled up and went outside. No wind. Only bright sunshine. She breathed deeply and looked toward the river where the sunlight had broken into silver pieces on the water. She squinted, turned away, and headed for the meadow.

The air was cool, almost spring-like. She grinned and spread her arms wide. Tiny wrens twitched in the bare blackberry bushes as she walked by. Two pairs of mallards moved away from India's side of the pond, their tiny wakes rippling toward the shore. Shiny green feathers covered the heads of the male ducks like exotic executioner hoods. Peculiar thought, India said to herself. She looked beyond the ducks to the east end of the pond. The swans floated peacefully in the still water.

India stopped and put her binoculars up to her eyes. She did not want to get much closer today—without the wind, the swans would easily hear her and fly away. Flying from pond to pond before and after their arctic trek was too stressful on them.

India's heart slowed as she watched the huge birds. She breathed deeply. One of the bigger white swans preened a smaller gray swan. The gesture seemed so tender. India did not like to anthropomorphize wild creatures. But couldn't wild things be tender? Couldn't they love? Who said those were strictly human attributes? Several swans floated in the water with their heads under—or within— their wings. The contorted position looked so comfortable. What would that be like to float on water, to sleep on water? Did the sleeping swan have to constantly tread water? Or did she just float?

India lowered the binoculars, then walked down the lane east through the meadow. She bent down when she got to the point at the cottonwood tree where the swans might be able to see her. She went around the gate toward the copse of evergreens. Then she decided to go toward the river, to be out in the middle of the meadow with its small rolling hills. The gorge cliffs towered to the south of her, across the river, the morning clouds shifting to reveal their unchanging rock faces. India bowed. A great blue heron flew above the Columbia River. Sea gulls seemed to have found erratic thermals and rode them, diving and dodging each other or some thing India could not see. Circling above her was a red-tailed hawk. She held her arms out and flew—Earthbound—with the hawk. She closed her eyes and tried to see through the hawk's eyes, to see the Earth from above.

She opened her eyes and watched the hawk do one more circle, then fly away toward Beacon Rock, which India could see from here. Once she had dreamed she was an eagle flying to Beacon Rock. She would see no bald eagles today. They would not return until February, about the same time she started seeing the red-winged blackbirds again. She was not certain where either species of bird went during the winter. All she knew is that the red-winged blackbirds left in the fall and returned to the backyard feeders mid-winter. Of course, maybe they never actually left; perhaps they went wherever birds go when it rains and stayed there until the bird feeders got too enticing.

India smiled. *Where do birds go when it rains*? What a question. Like where do all the socks go? You put a pair into the dryer and only one comes out. Do they end up in some great dryer in the sky?

India spotted something white on the ground and walked toward it. Two bones. One was stripped clean: immaculate white, straight, with two perfect holes at each end. India squatted. What animal did this belong to? It looked unreal. Probably a deer bone. She occasionally came across a deer carcass in this meadow. Downed by a coyote or mountain lion. The other bone still had gristle on one end. She knew some people collected bones. She stood. She wished she could collect bones. And feathers and stones. But she had heard that some birds used their dropped feathers like Hansel and Gretel used bread crumbs. And she did not want to destroy any habitats under stones by picking them up. After a storm or flooding, she would beachcomb and pick up driftwood and stones; she felt that these were gifts from the land that now needed taking. A form of beach cleaning.

India smiled as she gazed around her. Yes, this was bliss. This was paradise.

She walked toward the seven cottonwoods near the end of the pasture. Benjamin came through the gate at the far end. India waved.

What would they say to each other after last night?

India's feet bounced on the damp Earth. What did it matter? This seemed real, being here right now.

A moment later India and Benjamin stood facing one another on the cow path.

"Hello, India Lake."

India smiled. "Hello, Benjamin Swan. How did you sleep in your new digs?"

"Well, I felt kind of wimpy with the heat on."

India laughed. "Hey, I saw one of the swans preening a juvenile today."

Benjamin nodded. "I've noticed there is a difference in personalities. One couple is always preening and seeming to comfort a juvey. Others sleep a lot, especially when the wind is up. Then there is one who always seems on the lookout for trouble."

"That would be me," India said.

"Actually, there is one who reminds me of you," he said. "She's always off by herself, away from the crowd. She has a grayish head and neck, still pretty young. I'll show you when we get closer some time."

"I think I've seen her," India said. "Why does she remind you of me? Because she's alone?"

"She just seems to go her own way," Benjamin said.

"You want to walk?" India asked.

Benjamin nodded. India led them toward the seven cottonwoods.

"Last year I did some reading about the tundra and trumpeter swans," India said, "and they said their necks don't curve like the classic pictures we see of swans shaped like an S. But I've seen them with that curve quite a bit."

"But if you'll notice, their necks are generally straight, whereas the necks of the mute swans are curved almost always. You'd see the difference if you saw them together."

A hawk cried out. They both looked skyward.

"One more time," India said.

The hawk screeched a second time, then lifted off from one of the seven cottonwood trees.

"I can't fly," India called. "I wouldn't even have known you were there if you hadn't yelled at me."

Benjamin laughed.

"I like to keep up a dialogue with the local wildlife," India said. "I remember one day I was walking in the meadow, and I was wishing I was more a part of Nature. I felt so separate, as if I was in another world watching this world. Then suddenly I noticed the ducks swimming away from me, the red-winged blackbird announcing my arrival, a hawk screeching, and I just laughed at myself. Of course I was a part of it all. I couldn't be apart from it even if I tried. They weren't all streaming toward me like I was St. Francis, but that was because they are wild creatures. I want them to stay wild, too, so if being a part of it all means they view me as a predator and try to get away from me, that's just fine. Anyway, I didn't mean to interrupt you. We were talking about the S-shape. I wonder if that's one of the shapes in sacred geometry?"

They reached the seven cottonwoods. India put her hand out and touched one of them.

"If you think of an S as being part of the infinity shape," Benjamin said, "then the answer is yes."

"You've studied sacred geometry?" India asked.

He shook his head. "I've done a bit of reading." He looked up at the trees. India looked down. The ground was bare black from the cows' hooves.

"I call these trees the Seven Sisters," India said. "I'm not sure why. Like the Pleiades, maybe. They reminded me of forest nymphs dancing out here in the middle of the meadow. Kind of wild. I hate the thought of the cows trampling their roots and the ground, but maybe the trees like the company."

She shrugged. Benjamin was smiling. "What? You think I'm loony wondering about dancing trees and cavorting cows?"

"No, I like how your mind works. Can you tell me about your environmental group? Is it something to do with the swans?" He leaned against one of the cottonwood trees. His face looked a little drawn today, his eyes tired.

"Beth, you met her yesterday, used to go to all these meetings in the gorge, and there'd be sign-up sheets asking for name and organization. She started signing POOL for her organization: Pissed Off Old Ladies."

Benjamin laughed.

"A few years ago some of us got together when we realized the county was spraying our roads three times a year with dangerous pesticides," India said. "They wanted to do broadcast spraying for mosquitoes every two weeks. We needed a name for our group, so we took POOL, changing it to mean Pesticides Out of Our Lives. We've tried to work with the county, but they just condescended to us. Now we're considering a lawsuit. We have witnesses who say they have seen the guys from the county spraying water sources. Last year they did the mosquito spraying without getting an environmental impact statement, but fish and wildlife say they don't have anyone to enforce the laws. We want the county to come up with a different way to control weeds and other pests. They use more and more pesticides every year even though we have the same number of roads. You'd think that would give them a clue that the pesticides aren't effective. It's difficult to get people involved. They say it's too political. I say how can there be anything political about protecting our health: You're either for it or agin it! It's never that simple, I guess."

"You're not convinced?"

She shook her head. "I wish I owned all of this. Or some stretch of land. Then I could take care of it. I'd make certain no one poisoned or polluted it."

"But of course it doesn't work that way," Benjamin said.

"Because what someone does upstream or upwind or up the hill affects all the downstream, down wind, down river environments." India rubbed her face. "I'm tired of thinking about it. I don't think I can change the minds of people my age or older. Concrete brains. We've got to get the kids and try to reestablish that natural connection with nature. Did you do any environmental studies at your school?"

"In photography class, we did nature studies," Benjamin said, "but I've always been interested in creating an effective environmental program for children. That and ethics courses, to teach children ways to make decisions about what's right and wrong."

"Teaching them that money ain't everything," India said. "Heresy. As John Lennon says, 'We all want to change the world.'"

Benjamin smiled. "The world doesn't need changing."

"That's true," India said. "Just us. We need to become wilder."

"Wilder?"

"Yeah. Rooted. Part of. Like you." India twirled around slowly.

"Like me?"

"Yeah, you seem very rooted. Grounded."

"Huh," Benjamin said. "Thank you."

India stopped and smiled. "You and Jack OK?" It was none of her business but the words spilled out of her mouth anyway.

"Yes," Benjamin said. "I think we're OK."

India nodded.

"And how about you?" Benjamin said. "How do you feel about me this morning, I mean as your tenant and all?"

"I feel the same as I did before," India said, although she was not sure that was the truth. It had been fun fantasizing about this handsome stranger coming into her life. Now she was getting to know him: He had his own feelings, his own troubles. She wasn't sure she liked that—him being his own person. She grimaced at the thought. Raymond had once said he was a spear carrier in her life; he, himself, as a flesh and blood human being with his own identity did not exist for her.

"I have not had your terrible experiences," India said, "but living in a small town and trying to take on powerful forces has not been easy. I've been threatened. People have called me names and accused me of all kinds of misdeeds. At first it was awful. After a while, I just shrugged it off. I recognize I haven't had my job threatened, nor have I been hauled off to jail. I'm sure I wouldn't be so sanguine about it if that had happened. But I do know what it is like to be accused of sins you have not committed."

Benjamin looked off into the distance. They stood quietly together.

"I need to get into town," India finally said. "I better go."

Benjamin nodded.

"See you later, Benjamin," India said. She patted the tree and started to leave.

Benjamin walked alongside her. He cleared his throat, then said, "May I see you later?"

"I'm sure I'll see you later," she said. Her stomach lurched. What was he asking her?

"I'd like to spend time with you."

She glanced at him.

"I like spending time with you, too," India said.

Benjamin Swan stopped. India heard the murmurs of swans. She glanced toward the pond. One swan spread his wings wide, his head to the side, as if still waiting for that embrace.

"I haven't done this in years," Benjamin said. "I've forgotten how."

India looked at him.

"I'm attracted to you, India Lake. I would like to get to know you, woo you, court you, dance with you, whatever the right words would be."

India felt peculiar, fuzzy, as if none of this could be real. Why would Benjamin Swan be asking her out on a date? *Her*.

"Benjamin, I-I don't understand," I said.

"I haven't been with anyone for over seven years," Benjamin said. "I haven't even dated. It was my choice." He sighed. "There are reasons. But since I've met you, I think about you all of the time. Well, not all of the time, I'm not obsessed or anything."

India smiled and looked at the ground.

"I wondered if you felt anything similar?"

"Do you have some kind of disease?" India asked. "Is that why you've been celibate? Is that the right word? Were you a priest or something?" India took off her hat and loosened her scarf. The sun was getting warm.

"No, I've always gotten along with women, but when I got into relationships it seemed like it wasn't the real me they cared about. It was some ideal. Or some thing that was not who I was. I can't explain it."

"And now you want to go out with me?" India said. "Why? You thought you'd find some old gray haired lady you'd break your fast with?"

Benjamin stepped back from her. "What? No, where did that come from?"

"Benjamin, look at me."

"I have looked at you. For days. Weeks."

"Look again. This is who I am. I'm on the other side of forty. I piss off easily. I don't wear make-up, or shave any part of my body, and my bags have bags. I'm not interested in becoming someone else. I'm not going to suddenly dye my hair blond or wax my legs. This is it. Is this what you want to get to know better?" She heard the anger in her voice. She knew it was not all directed at him, but there it was.

"You are not *what* I want to get to know better. You are *who* I want to know."

"I don't want to be anyone's special project," India said. "When I told you the other night that I wanted to be wanted it was not an invitation to feel sorry for me."

"What have I said to offend you? That I like you? That you're beautiful?"

"When I said I wanted to be wanted," India said, looking at the sky. "I meant I wanted someone to want me so much—"

"—that his knees nearly buckle when you come into a room? That he pressed his face in your pillow just to get a scent of you?"

"Now that's weird," India said.

Benjamin laughed. India smiled. He reached for her hand.

"What smell?" India asked. She didn't wear perfume.

"Earth. You smell like the Earth." He pulled her toward him. "Like home." She looked up at him, and they kissed. His mustache tickled her lips.

"That's scratching me—" she began.

He kissed her again. This time her knees felt weak. He put his arm around her waist and held her up. Still they kissed.

India pulled away, dazed. "I've got to meet Beth." She backed away.

"India."

"Come to the house at six. No, five. We'll—we'll talk then."

She hurried away from Benjamin Swan and the pond without a backward glance.

CHAPTER EIGHT

DANIEL SALMONSON AND Beth were already eating when India got to the Crossroads. Daniel did not look like any lawyer India had ever met before. When he was not in court, he dressed in jeans and a white shirt. His light brown hair was pulled back into a ponytail, and he always looked like he had a headache.

"Sorry I'm late," India said, pulling out a chair and sitting in it. "Hi, Daniel, Beth."

"Look who's here," Beth said softly to India.

India glanced across the tiny dining room. Andrew Stephenson sat with Dick Lament. The first was the prosecuting attorney who also acted as the county's attorney, the second was the commissioner for India's end of the county.

"I'm hoping Andrew will note the fact that we're having lunch with the best environmental lawyer in the state of Washington."

"You want anything, Indy?" Clementine leaned over the counter and called to her. "I've got Venus' Vegetable soup."

India turned around. "Is the soup vegetarian?" she asked.

"It's got a little chicken stock," Clementine said.

"That's like being a little pregnant," India said.

"You trying to tell us something, Indy?" Clementine asked, grinning.

"Nothing for me today," India said.

"Okey dokey."

Clementine turned back to the kitchen.

Andrew glanced up from his meal and caught India's gaze. They nodded to one another. India had talked to Andrew when they first suspected the county was spraying water sources. He was the prosecuting attorney, and since the applicator was a county employee, Andrew was his attorney. He refused to pursue the case. India called the state attorney general's office and asked if they would look into it. The AG office said they only investigated cases recommended to them by prosecuting attorneys.

"But it's the prosecuting attorney who is the problem. He has a conflict of interest," India told the assistant at the AG office.

"Even so," the assistant said. She felt like she had been dropped into Catch-22 land.

"I was reminding Beth that just because someone has been wronged does not mean someone else is going to hand over some money," Daniel said. "I haven't exactly figured out who our class is for this class action suit. Who is the county harming? These kinds of charges are very difficult to prove. If they are following the directions on the labels, they'll say they are blameless for any harm."

"Can't we sue on behalf of the environment, the fish, birds, frogs, and us? They sprayed Marlo's property, and she wasn't notified even though she's on the pesticide sensitive list."

"They compensated her," Daniel said.

India made a noise.

"Besides, we don't want money," India said. "We want them to change their policies."

"It rarely works that way," Daniel said. "I have done some checking and there do seem to be some irregularities. I'm willing to go forward, but for something like this, I really need a retainer."

"I thought we'd pay you after we win," India said. "Contingency."

"I do that sometimes," Daniel said, "but on something like this, I can't afford to go gratis."

"Can't you just threaten the county with a lawsuit to get them to change their policies?" Beth asked.

He shrugged. "That didn't work with Marlo's case. Granted, this is bigger. I can put some research together and write a letter, but I still need the retainer."

"How much?" India asked.

"$10,000."

India's mouth fell open. Beth looked at her plate.

"That's actually cheap for what you're asking me to

commit to. I don't think there's much precedent suing on behalf of the environment. But I'm willing to take a look."

"POOL hasn't any money," India said. "None of us does."

"We'll try and figure something out," Beth said.

"Jack Combs just told me they're considering trading the Dutch property for some property near Indian Heaven owned by Aviary Lumber," India said. "They say they won't develop it."

"They can't develop it," Daniel said. "It's outside any city limits so it falls under the purview of the Scenic Act. They could clear-cut, but there aren't any trees to speak of to clear-cut."

"Do you know anything about Aviary Lumber?"

Daniel shook his head. "I'll do some checking," he said. "I've got to be in court in Vancouver in an hour." Daniel stood. "I'll talk to you soon." He put some money on the table, nodded to Andrew, then left.

Beth sighed. "Well, that's that."

Clementine came over and sat with them. "So are you going to sue the county?" Clementine occasionally attended POOL meetings.

"We need $10,000," India said. "Got some?"

"You could have a bake sale," Clementine suggested. "A really big bake sale."

"That's an idea," Beth said. "We shouldn't give up yet. We're having our next meeting next Wednesday, Clemmy. Can you attend? We're having it early, so it doesn't conflict with the holidays. We'll brainstorm ideas."

India looked over at the prosecuting attorney and commissioner. She was tempted to stick out her tongue.

"Hell hath no fury like a pissed off old lady," India said. She got up.

"India," Beth said.

India walked over to the table.

"Hello, gentlemen."

"Hello, India," they both said.

"Have you given any more thought to hiring an Integrated Pest Management consultant so you can figure out other ways to control pests besides spewing poison everywhere?"

"Now, India," Dick Lament said in his most patronizing voice. "Everything we use is perfectly legal."

"And listed on the EPA's pesticide lists as very hazardous," India said. "One of the chemicals you use is linked to testicular cancer, Dick. The other one is harmful to the salmonids, in direct violation of the Endangered Species Act. That's a federal violation. We think it's time you good ol' boys got some good ol' common sense. We're going to figure out a way to sue you, and we won't settle for a mere $8,000 like Marlo was forced to do, or $5,000 like that woman who was sexually harassed accepted. We're talking *class action lawsuit*, boys."

"India, you have no basis—"

"You know, Andrew, you are supposed to be the *people's* advocate. I wish you'd start acting like it instead of finding legal loopholes to get these assholes out of their messes. Start standing up for us. You've got kids. Pesticides aren't good for their little immune systems."

Somebody put a hand on India's shoulder. She whirled around. Beth.

"Dear, I have to get going now," she said.

Andrew and Dick Lament stood. Lament peeled money off a wad and left it on the table.

"Thanks for lunch, Clem," Dick said. "Beth, India."

The two men walked by the women and out the door.

"I'll see you later," Beth said. She followed the men out.

"India, those were eating, paying customers," Clementine said.

"Sorry," India said.

They were alone in the restaurant. India and Clementine began collecting the dirty dishes."

"The thing is, India," Clementine said, "things happen slowly."

"Why is that?" India asked. "Why do good things happen slowly and bad things happen quickly?"

Clementine shrugged. "That's just the way it is."

They took the dishes into the kitchen.

"Hey, your ears must have been burning this morning," Clementine said as she wiped down the stainless steel counters. "Jack and Benjamin were here really early. I tried not to listen, but it's a small place."

"You know Benjamin?"

"Sure, he comes in here quite often," she said. "Here, eat this apple. It's organic. You look like you need the sugar. Anyway, I think Benjamin was asking if it was all right with Jack if he went out with you."

"Oh gawd."

"If it was all right with you, of course. He didn't want to hurt Jack or go behind his back, you know. He wanted to make sure it was cool with him. I guess he knows you and Jack still sleep together."

"Geez. Does everyone in town know?"

"Probably." Clementine rinsed the dish rag, folded it, and hung it on the faucet.

"I'm not sleeping with him," India said. "It's been weeks. Maybe months."

"I haven't had sex with Sammy in—hmmm, nine months. Yeah. Our anniversary. But we're still sleeping together."

"You're married to each other. Jack and I are friends. Besides, he's dating Violet now."

"Really? I was thinking of going to her belly dancing class. You been?"

"Yes," India said. "What's the rest of the story with Benjamin and Jack?"

Clementine laughed. "He is gorgeous, though I'm partial to fat and bald myself. Tell *me*, what's the rest of the story?" Clementine folded her arms across her chest and smiled at India. India washed the apple, dried it on Clementine's apron, then bit into it.

India wanted to tell someone, but she could not imagine what it would sound like out loud: Local librarian lusts after Swan Knight.

"Benjamin did ask if he could see me," India said. "Date me, whatever. I didn't know what to say. I mean look at him and look at me."

Clementine frowned. "What are you talking about?

You're beautiful."

India snorted. "You haven't looked at a magazine lately, have you."

"No, and why are you? Why are you talking about yourself like he's Prince Charming and you're the ugly duckling or Cinderella who never meets her fairy god-mother. That's not your style."

India shrugged. "Lately I feel strange. Like I did everything wrong in my life. Every thing pisses me off. I'm lusting after strangers. Kissing them in the middle of cow pastures."

"Really. You're kissing strang*ers* in a cow pasture? Is there a line of strangers waiting to kiss you?"

"Very funny," India said.

"Don't worry about it," Clementine said. "Just try to go with it. You're getting older. You don't have the same tolerance for bullshit as you used to. Comes with the gray hair." Clementine gave India a hug. "So go have some fun."

"Thanks," India said. "Maybe I will."

INDIA STOOD IN the middle of her living room. Benjamin was coming out soon. For what? She had said they would talk. About what? He wanted to get to know her better. Good luck, she thought. She didn't even know herself much these days. Had she ever? She knew her opinions on issues and ideas. Was that who she was? Her job was not who she was, she knew that. Was this land where she lived who she was?

She rubbed her arms. Had Raymond known who she

Kim Antieau

was? Did relationships really begin with people getting to know one another? Or did it start with lust and then they got to know each other just enough to be able to tolerate one another. Coupledom was achieved. Then each partner began taking over the chores and activities the other one did not want to do. "That's all right darling. I'll do it for you." Raymond didn't like confrontation or doing the bills, so India handled the money and any disputes that popped up over the course of a life together. India did not like cooking or entertaining, so Raymond became the chef and the social one in the partnership. Until they each began to resent the other's burdens.

How does one maintain a separate self and still be in a relationship?

Wait! India thought. She did not want a *relationship*. She did not want to *talk*. She did not want Benjamin Swan to get to know her better.

Why had she asked him over anyway? Maybe she could pretend she had forgotten, that she was not home.

A knock at the door.

India went to the door and opened it. Benjamin stood on her threshold dressed in jeans and a T-shirt. He held out a white feather to her.

"I found it near the pond," he said. "It's a swan feather."

India took the proffered gift. Her fingers shook slightly.

"Thank you," she said. "Come in."

He stepped into the room. She closed the door. She turned to set the feather on the countertop, and he put his arms around her waist and leaned down to kiss her neck. Her breath caught in her throat. She put her arms behind her and reached for him, pulling him against her. She turned her mouth to him. She could barely stand as they kissed. Could not think. Only felt.

"There is something about you," she said, pulling away, catching her breath. They walked to the couch.

"I've wanted you since the first time we met," Benjamin whispered.

India lay on the couch. Benjamin kissed her neck, cheek, mouth. India took off his T-shirt. She kissed his bare chest, his nipples. Breathed him into her lungs. He smelled like air and fire, dancing together. She unbuttoned her shirt.

"It's been a long time," he whispered. "I might—"

"I don't care," she said. She did not remember ever feeling quite this way before. Overcome? No. Every cell seemed to vibrate. "Do you have any diseases I need to worry about catching?"

"No, you, me?"

"No," she said. She pulled off her slacks and camisole. She lay naked beneath him.

"You are so beautiful," he whispered.

She unbuttoned his jeans.

He stood, unzipped his jeans, and stepped out of them and his underwear. India reached for him. She opened her legs, guided him in. She was wet, and he slipped inside of her easily. They moved quickly against one another.

"I can't wait," Benjamin said. "I'm sorry."

India barely heard him, barely knew anything except

her desire.

"Don't stop," she breathed. "Just don't stop."

"India, India."

She moved her hips, dug her fingers into his butt, pulled him against her, until he pulsed inside her, massaging her to orgasm, his back arching as they came together.

Breathing heavily, they looked at each other. And started laughing.

"No, don't," she said, opening her legs farther. "I want you to stay inside of me."

He leaned on his elbows and looked at her.

"So much for talk," she said.

"And getting to know each other."

"What better way to get acquainted?" India said. "I don't think that's ever happened, Benjamin. Coming at the same time the first time." She felt him shrinking inside of her. She moved her hips.

"That feels nice," he whispered. He kissed her mouth. "I guess we were both ready."

India grinned. "Let's see if we can move without you falling out. I feel you getting hard again. I want to get on top of you."

They slowly moved together until India was on top of Benjamin. She looked down at him, at her pubic hair and his penis. She moved her hips in a figure eight. Her fingers traced the outside of Benjamin's nipples. Benjamin grew harder. India leaned over and kissed his nipples. They moved together. She had to keep catching her breath; it felt so exquisite to have him inside of her. He put his hands on her hips and gently pushed up inside her.

Her hips created sacred shapes while he moved beneath her. Benjamin put his thumb on her stretched clitoris as he pushed up into her. She gasped.

"That's too intense," she whispered.

"Do you want me to stop?"

"No, no, no."

How could she feel so much pleasure everywhere? It was almost as if Benjamin wasn't there—as if the Universe itself was making love to her.

She danced her dance around his penis until they both started to orgasm. Then she moved faster, harder on him, pushed away his fingers, and moved so her clitoris rubbed his belly. His orgasm massaged her vagina with ecstasy again. Then she came alone, crying out, "Yayayayaya!" and laughing as she came off the ceiling and fell face down onto Benjamin's chest.

They breathed heavily together for several minutes. Then India raised her head for a moment and said, "So there you are."

Benjamin slipped out of her. He wrapped his arms around her naked body, and they fell to sleep.

CHAPTER NINE

INDIA OPENED HER eyes. Sweat was beginning to cool from her body. She felt sticky. She looked up at Benjamin. His eyes were closed. She saw a piece of white in his black beard. She reached up and gently picked it off. Was that what the swans did when they preened one another? Were they finding pieces of black to pick out?

India slowly sat up.

"India," Benjamin whispered, reaching for her.

"I'll be back," she said.

She padded to the bathroom and stood in front of the mirror. Same ol' broad. What had she been thinking? She smiled. She hadn't been thinking.

She leaned into the shower and turned on the water. She put her hands up to her face. She smelled him on her. She stared at the water. If she stepped in there, she would wash him all away. Would he then disappear from the couch? From her thoughts? Was he only a delicious fantasy?

No. He was a man.

And she was going to start to stink if she didn't shower.

Benjamin knocked on the bathroom door.

"Come," India said.

The door opened.

Benjamin filled the doorway, so tall and naked.

"I-I couldn't decide if I should shower or not," India said.

He looked at her face, then at her entire body, taking her all in, she thought, like someone soaking up the sun or gazing at moonlight.

Or like someone who was truly seeing her.

Steam drifted out of the shower.

"We could go together," Benjamin said. "Unless you want to be alone."

"No," India said, reaching for him. "Stay."

"CAN I READ something you've written?" Benjamin asked. He stood in the kitchen. India sat at the counter.

"No. First you must feed me."

"OK. What would you like me to make?" Benjamin asked.

India suddenly saw her ex, Raymond, in her mind's eye hunched over the chopping board, her sitting at their kitchen table running the adding machine.

"Let's do it together," India said, getting up and coming to stand next to him. "How about some scrambled eggs and toast? That's easy. Bowl's up there." India pointed. She opened the refrigerator and took out four eggs. Benjamin reached up and got down a glass bowl. India cracked the eggs, one at a time, and dropped them into the bowl. Benjamin stood behind her and got a fork from the dish rack. India watched his hand as he used the fork to break the golden yolks and scramble them until they were bright yellow. She breathed deeply. Benjamin's smell filled her nostrils. She put her hand on his right arm. He kissed the top of her head. She leaned back until their bodies touched. Benjamin set the fork against the inside of the glass bowl, then cupped his hands over her belly and kissed her neck.

India let go of Benjamin's arm, got bread from the refrigerator, and put four slices in the toaster oven. Benjamin opened the cupboard and took down the olive oil.

India smiled. "Good guess."

Benjamin moved the skillet already on the stove to the front burner and switched it on. India poured a little olive oil into the pan. Benjamin and India stood side by side, the hairs on their arms just touching. When the oil was hot, India picked up the skillet and turned it so that the oil moved from its small circle to coat the bottom of the pan. Benjamin poured the eggs into the skillet.

"Let's hope the swans never find out we eat eggs," India said.

Benjamin laughed.

"THIS IS THE novel," India said, handing Benjamin *Nature Girl*. "This shelf has copies of all of my published short stories."

"And you're just giving this up?"

"No, not completely. It's just not a passion anymore. I feel punch drunk—too many rejections. I did it for twenty years. Now maybe something else will come up. You can read it if you like. Don't worry. I won't ask if you like it."

"Do you miss writing?"

She shrugged. "I try not to think about it." She swallowed. "Something I loved doing. I loved telling stories. I loved creating the worlds and characters. I loved spending time with them." She grimaced. "Easier than real life, I suppose."

"Or maybe it was a different kind of real life," he said. "Art has truth in it, I believe. You tell your truth through stories."

"Maybe. What I want to do, what I always try to do, is convey a reverence for the natural world. My love for it. That's difficult. Writing about true passion and really getting someone else to understand it is a Herculean task. I wish I could do Nature writing. I'd love that. I read Terry Tempest Williams and other Nature writers, and I am in awe of their abilities. I stand in the meadow and try to describe what I see and how I feel and all I can think of is, wow, this is beautiful."

"Words can't always do it," Benjamin said. "The Universe existed before words."

"So I've been told," India said. "Rhonda says dance

existed before there were words."

India switched off the light, and they returned to the living room. She took the book from Benjamin's hand and set it on the counter. She put her arms around his waist.

"Shall we dance and see if we need any words?" India asked.

Benjamin put his arms around her, and they danced, slowly, in a circle. She liked the feel of his body in her arms. The familiar unfamiliarity of it. And his smell. She put her face against his chest and breathed deeply. They should bottle it. He pulled her camisole out of her slacks and put his hands on her bare waist.

India leaned her head back and looked at him.

"Maybe the third time we'll get it right?"

"You mean we did it wrong before?" he asked, smiling.

"Let's try the bed."

IT TOOK LONGER this time. India lay beneath Benjamin with her legs opened wide, wanting him to fall deeply into her. He looked into her eyes as they rocked together. She felt his testicles against her cunt as his penis moved in and almost out of her. He stayed hard as she came. Then he kept moving inside her. Slower. And then faster. Their bodies undulated together. Until India came again. Exhausted, she held onto Benjamin until he climaxed. Then they lay against each other, India's inner thighs aching, each breathing the other's breath.

They shifted until they were facing each other on their

sides.

"If I wrote this in a book, my friend Nancy wouldn't believe it," India said. "She says my characters have great sex, and that is unbelievable."

Benjamin chuckled. "I'm not sure what she means."

"She says, to quote, that my characters get on, get off, and get off. She says I should show my characters having lousy sex."

"Hmmm."

"Yeah, I suppose that says a lot about both of our sex lives," India said. "I've never had trouble getting off, so to speak."

"Not a problem for me either."

India laughed. "With women it's different, or so they say. We're more in our heads."

"I don't know," Benjamin said. "You seemed in your body."

"Yeah, it's the so-called experts who say women aren't in their bodies. I wonder if that's just more bullshit about women—some kind of fear-based analysis. Can you imagine how powerful women would be if we truly inhabited our bodies. We'd be full of ourselves. And fully sexual. For some reason that scares society. I am woman, hear me come!"

Benjamin laughed.

"How was it, Benjamin Swan, after a seven year hiatus? Are you glad you broke your fast?"

"I never had trouble with the sex part," Benjamin said. "I've always known how to please. It was afterward."

"Wow. You had sex like this all of the time? How

could you give it up?"

"No, I didn't have sex like this. This was wonderful. This was—you make me feel wild. Before I never felt as though anyone saw my soul. The true me. It's hard to explain."

"Would you really want someone to see your soul?"

"Yes," Benjamin said. "I want you to see my soul."

"Isn't that a private thing, something to be protected, nourished?" India asked. "If someone sees who you really are, aren't you exposed, vulnerable?"

"But then if you are loved, you know you are truly loved for your being. Not just outward appearances."

They lay in the darkness together. India heard a clock ticking somewhere.

Benjamin sat up. "That's enough for tonight. I'm taking your book and going back to the garage."

"Stay," she whispered.

He kissed her mouth.

"May I see you in the morning?" he asked.

"Yes, you may."

Drowsily India listened to Benjamin dress in the darkness, heard him whisper good night. She thought about getting up and making sure the door was locked, but she remembered Benjamin was the Swan Knight. He would not forget to lock the door.

She grinned and fell to sleep.

INDIA AWAKENED TO sunlight. She blinked and lifted up her blankets. She was naked. She slowly sat up. Her right knee throbbed and her crotch hurt. She threw off the covers and got up. She limped into the bathroom. When she peed, it burned slightly. She turned on the water and stepped into the shower.

She screamed at the shock of the cold water and jumped out of the shower. She stood dripping on the cold stone floor for a moment.

The spell had been broken.

She adjusted the water temperature, then stepped back into the shower. What had happened last night? What had she been thinking? Penises, vaginas, erections, cunts, wet spots. She had had more sex in a couple of hours last night than she usually had in a year. More than Benjamin Swan had had in seven years. They had not even used protection.

She covered her face with her hands. That would be great. A single pregnant forty-five year old town librarian.

She was going to have to see him again. This morning. Face him. Remember what they had done. How she had felt.

She still felt him draining out of her.

She let the water pour over her.

Maybe he had awakened with similar thoughts.

She finished her shower, got dressed, and went into the living room. She stopped and looked around. They had left the living and kitchen area a mess. Now it was tidy, cushions off the floor, dishes washed and dried in the rack.

Someone knocked. India went and answered the door. Benjamin stood on her threshold, her novel in hand.

"This is wonderful," he said, stepping into the house. "I stayed up all night reading it."

"Good morning."

He smiled, put his arms around her, and looked into her eyes. "Good morning." He kissed her lips. Butterflies tickled her stomach.

Apparently Benjamin Swan had not had any second thoughts. Of course, he had not been to sleep yet.

He strode into the room. "You can't quit. This was exquisite."

India took the book from him. "Your review would have more weight if you weren't sleeping with the author."

"*Au contraire*," Benjamin said. "Perhaps if I'd flattered you before we made love. Not that I would have consciously tried to lure you into bed with raves of your writing."

India laughed. "Well, I'm glad you liked it."

"No, India, listen. It is a powerful story. A girl alone in the world who finds her way only after connecting with Nature—becoming Nature in a way. Very moving. Wouldn't it be great to let go of our inhibitions that way? To really be free to be ourselves?"

His face glowed as he spoke. India smiled.

"You seemed rather uninhibited last night," India said. "Free."

Benjamin grinned. "I felt that way. I still feel that way. You?"

India laid the paperback on the counter and went into the kitchen.

"India?"

Benjamin followed her.

"You hungry?" India asked.

Benjamin looked at her.

"Well," she said. "I did feel a little strange this morning. I've never done what we did before. I mean, we're practically strangers having unprotected sex all over the house."

"India, I've had sex with three women in my entire life—four including you—and that was seven years ago. The women are all still healthy. All married with children."

"I haven't had sex with anyone but Jack in five years. Same with him, I'm pretty sure. I made him get tested before I'd sleep with him."

Benjamin put a hand on the counter. "Jack and you have been monogamous for five years? That sounds serious. You both act like it was nothing. I'm not sure—I'm not sure what that means."

"It means we were comfortable and safe being with each other, but we weren't in love."

"He was, India," Benjamin said. "He told me. He said he resigned himself to being your friend and occasionally having some friendly sex."

"You know, I don't appreciate other people discussing my sex life." She breathed deeply. "I don't want to fight. I was trying to tell you I was scared. I am scared. I don't want to feel like I'm sixteen again, trembling, while I wait for my boyfriend to come over. I've worked hard to be an individual, to be independent. I don't want to fall into you. I don't want to disappear."

"I don't want that either," Benjamin said.

"But it's different for you," India said. "You're a man. Everyone I've ever been with seemed charmed with me until I was *his*, quote unquote. Then I was supposed to fit into them. Adam's rib. I won't do that. It's death, Benjamin."

"I don't want you to disappear," Benjamin said. "Don't you think I'm afraid? I'm homeless, for chrissake, jobless, living in a tent in the the middle of a marsh, wondering what the hell happened to my life. Then I meet you and I panic. How can I convince this wonderful woman to see me? I was so afraid you'd look at me and see homeless, jobless, accused pornographer child molester. I keep waiting for your eyes to change. I saw it happen so many times last winter."

India sighed. "It's good that we've started off as two whole healthy people. I was going to make oatmeal. You want some?"

"All right." Benjamin took a deep breath. "So are we OK?"

"Yes, let's just take this slow and easy," India said, getting the oatmeal from the cupboard.

"Whew, guess it's a good thing we didn't have sex on our first date."

"Yeah, good thing."

AFTER BREAKFAST, BENJAMIN and India went to the meadow. It was warm and sunny. India wore a jacket instead of her winter coat. They stayed at the west end of the pond and pointed camera and binoculars at the swans who had flocked to the east end. Today most dug around the edges of the pond, looking for food. As India watched the birds from afar, she heard the click, click, click of Benjamin's camera.

"That's the first time I've seen you with your camera," India said. Two of the swans floated next to one another, necks straight, black beaks parallel to the water. They looked like mirror images of one another. Or twins.

"You inspired me," he said, glancing at her, then looking back through the viewfinder. "As I was reading your book I thought, she can't stop. Then I realized I had stopped, too. Punishing the world by not doing what I love. That doesn't make sense."

"Stories are different than pictures. Stories are meant to be heard," India said. "If no one reads or hears a story you've created it feels like a kind of death. Like you've failed. I can't keep writing stories that never get heard. It's as if I'm destroying something wild. When I write, I feel as though I am connecting to something primal, wild, and when no one gets to hear or read these creations, it's like they die."

"I'd love to read what you'd have to say about the swans. Retell the Swan Maiden story. Or whatever. You have a kind of ecstasy of language."

"I'll write about the swans, and you can take the pictures. We'll get it published and use part of the proceeds to pay the lawyer to sue the county."

Benjamin looked at her. "Would that work?"

"No. First we'd have to find a publisher. That takes a

long time. If it gets accepted, we'd have to wait to actually get it published. Then we'd only get a tiny percentage. For my novel I got about a dollar per copy sold. One dollar. Which might be nice if I sold a million copies, but I didn't. Anyway, it wouldn't all happen fast enough unless we did it ourselves."

"Let's do it anyway," Benjamin said. "You haven't seen my work yet, but I am pretty good. You said you've wanted to do nature writing."

"You don't have to figure out things for me to do," India said. "I don't need rescuing from my horrendous existence."

"It's selfish," he said. "I want to read what you have to say about swans."

"Then just listen," India said. She began dancing in circles around him. "I love them! They are *magnifique!* Stupendous! Loverly!"

Benjamin took her outstretched hand, and India whirled beneath his arm. Then she held out her hand, and he ducked under her hand as he twirled. He laughed. She smiled. She was not sure she had ever met a grown man so free with his emotions. His delights. She liked it. They twirled until they were in each other's arms.

"It might be fun to work together," Benjamin said.

"It would give us an excuse to be together," India said, "without the entire town speculating on our relationship."

Benjamin raised his eyebrows.

"OK. So they're already speculating."

"Let me show you my pictures."

"All right," she agreed.

They let go of each other and headed back to India's garage. Benjamin held India's hand, and she let him. She could not remember the last time she had held hands with a man for more than a second. High school? College?

Once inside the small room above the garage, Benjamin opened his laptop.

"These are just some throwaway shots I took."

"No excuses," India said. "Just show me." She leaned closer to the computer screen.

In the first photograph a swan opening her wings filled the screen. She looked huge, powerful, and graceful. Mist seemed to eddy around her. The next photo was of a gray swan, his neck arched over another adult swan as he attempted to feed at the water's edge. The next was of the whole brood dining on mud.

"These are very expressive," India said. "Artistic rather than wholly realistic. It is as if I am looking at another world very much like this one only—only filled with fairy dust. It makes me want to write a fairy tale just looking at these. They are quite wonderful."

"Thank you," he said. "So you'll think about a joint project?"

"Sure," she said. "You have plans for lunch?"

He closed the computer and twined his fingers with hers. Her knees felt wobbly. She looked into his eyes.

"I don't know," she whispered. "I think you broke me last night."

He kissed her forehead. "I doubt it."

Benjamin led her to his sleeping bag on the floor.

"Oh, no, Benjamin. Remember, I'm not a good camper."

He opened the sleeping bag and motioned for her to sit.

"Yes, sir."

He unzipped her jacket and took it off. Then he slipped off her socks and shoes. He kissed each toe. Took off her blouse, her jeans.

"Are you warm enough?" he asked.

She nodded.

He lifted her camisole over her head and kissed her breasts. Then he kissed her mouth. She lay back. He slowly removed her panties. He kissed her mouth, between her breasts, her belly. His hand ran up the inside of her thigh. She moaned. His lips reached her cunt, his tongue found her clitoris. She put her hand on his head. She wanted him to stop. And to continue. She closed her eyes, opened her legs. She was getting wetter and wetter. She arched her back, almost climaxing, and his tongue slowed, then moved faster, slower.

She heard him open his pants even as he licked her. She was coming, coming—then he stopped and he was up inside of her suddenly, easily. She gasped. Felt his clothes against her bare skin, him inside of her. She was sliding with the sleeping bag, but Benjamin put up his hand to stop them from hitting the wall as they moved deeper and deeper into each other.

Until they climaxed seconds from one another.

Benjamin gently moved out of India. He kissed her mouth.

"Wow," she said. "Guess I'm not broke."

"Guess not."

She tugged at his clothes. "Not fair."

"I couldn't wait," he said into her ear. "I had to touch you, had to have you in my mouth."

She felt dreamy as she looked at him. "This can't last," she whispered. "It won't always be like this."

"So? And who says, anyway?"

"I'm hungry," India said. "I said I wanted lunch, not sex."

"Isn't it nice you're going to get both."

CHAPTER TEN

"DO YOU WANT to come to the meeting with me tonight?" India asked as she and Benjamin finished lunch.

"What meeting?"

"The state is thinking of trading the turtle pond for some other property."

Benjamin leaned over the table and kissed India's mouth. "If you're there, I'm there."

India laughed. She had never been with anyone who was so . . . there. She was not quite sure what to do with all the attention. She glanced at Benjamin. How much longer could it last?

"What's wrong?" he asked, trying to meet her gaze.

She shook her head as she stood. "I'm just ready to do these dishes."

INDIA AND BENJAMIN arrived at the commissioners' meeting room a few minutes before the seven o'clock start time. Most of the other POOLers were already there. Jack sat behind the empty commissioners' table at the front of the room. He nodded at India, frowned, then looked back down at his notebook. India and Benjamin sat next to Rhonda and Isaac. Nancy and Marian came in after and sat behind them.

"Where's Deb?" India asked Nancy.

"She had to work," Nancy said, "but she sends her support. Whatever is good for the swans and turtles, etc."

India sighed. She hated meetings, especially when the commissioners were involved. They were so clearly looking after their own best interests that she could barely stand to be in the same building with them. Other meetings with other governmental entities were almost as bad. They asked for public input but did what they wanted anyway. She hoped Jack was right about Aviary Lumber.

At 7:05, the three commissioners filed into the room along with two people India did not recognize. She glanced at Benjamin. He looked strange. Pale. Suddenly stiff.

Jack stood and said, "Thank you all for coming, and we especially thank the commissioners for letting us use their meeting room. I'm Jack Combs, the Refuge manager. This is Bryant Willard, my boss. He's been coordinating the proposed trade between the park service and

Aviary Lumber. Bryant?"

Jack sat as Bryant Willard stood.

"Good evening..."

India shifted in her seat as he began his spiel. She glanced around the room. She knew most of the people. A man in the back wearing an expensive suit was not familiar. One of their lawyers? She looked back at Willard as he introduced the public relations manager of Aviary Lumber. She missed his name but listened as he extolled the virtues of the exchange—the transfer, they called it. He promised not to cut or plant trees for future timber harvest. He said their company was "committed to protecting the land," especially the turtle pond.

Then Dick Lament spoke for the commissioners and county, saying simply, "We need the land back on our tax roles."

They called for questions. Rhonda and Nancy asked the most. India glanced at Benjamin again. He looked so uncomfortable.

"What's wrong?" India whispered.

"It's just stuffy in here," he said. "I think I'll wait outside."

"OK."

He got up. India watched him leave. The man in the back looked at Benjamin and then over at her. She stared at him for a moment, then looked forward again.

". . . we hope to phase out the cattle within a year of the transfer," the Aviary man was saying.

India raised her hand. The man nodded to her.

"Why are you doing this? What's the advantage to

your company?"

"Good question," the PR man said.

India rolled her eyes. Could he be more patronizing?

Dick Lament leaned over to the PR man and whispered something. The man nodded.

"I guess he just informed him about your rap sheet," Beth said.

India smiled. "Yeah, I'm sure."

"We're doing it to help our corporate image," he said. "I have to be honest with you. This looks good for us. And we want to walk the walk as well as talk the talk."

"But you're a lumber company," India said. "There aren't many trees at Turtle Pond."

"Actually," the man said, "our official corporate moniker is Aviary *Building* Company. We know the ABC's of home building." He smiled and nodded, a beaming advertisement for his company.

Jack caught India's eye. She smiled. He shrugged. She glanced over at the door. The man in the suit was gone.

Nancy leaned forward so that her head was between Rhonda and India.

"What do you think?" she whispered.

"They're wrapping themselves in the green flag all right," Rhonda said. "But is it for real?"

"If the commissioners are for it," India said, "I'm suspicious. Daniel Salmonson said he'd look into the company."

"Any more questions?" the Aviary man asked.

The meeting dragged on for another half hour. When they finally adjourned—after promising another meeting before the final decision—India waited for Jack while the room cleared.

"What'd you think?" Jack asked.

"Can we believe what they say?" India asked.

"The Park Service has exchanged land with them before," Jack said. "And they did what they said they would do."

Jack and India walked into the darkness. Cars pulled out of the parking lot. India waved to Isaac and Rhonda as they went by. She looked around for Benjamin and didn't see him.

"You want to go out for coffee?" Jack asked as they walked to India's car. A piece of paper fluttered under her windshield wiper. She lifted the wiper blade and picked the paper off of the glass.

"Got a ride home. See you later. B.," she read.

She looked at Jack. "Where would we get coffee at this time of night in Shahalla, if I actually drank coffee?"

Jack smiled. "My house."

India laughed. "You're cute, Jack. I thought you were dating Violet."

"So?" Jack said.

India unlocked her car.

"Just two friends hanging out together," he said.

India opened the door and got in.

"It's too cold for this discussion," she said.

Jack leaned into the door.

"My house is nice and cozy," he said.

She smiled. Why was she hesitating? Why hadn't she

slammed the car door on him? Because he was Jack, her longtime friend and sometime lover. Something about him was so comfortable. Familiar. She felt in control. Even when they had sex. It was good. Fun. Orgasmic. But she did not feel as though she was about to...what? Lose control.

Jack grinned. India reached up and grabbed his coat and pulled him down to her. She kissed him on the mouth, then let him go.

"Give it up, Jack," she said.

Jack laughed and stepped away from the car. She shut the door, started the car, and drove away. She felt her face reddening.

Why had she done that? She had just suddenly wanted him. For a moment she had longed for how it had been when they were first together. Never like it was with her and Benjamin. But nice. They had liked each other. They had been immediate old friends. Until they drifted away from each other.

India drove down SR14. She wondered why Benjamin had disappeared. And who had taken him home? She knew so little about him. Except how wonderful his body felt against hers.

She smiled. Right now, that was all she needed to know.

INDIA SAT AT her kitchen table listening to the clock tick. She expected Rhonda soon. Time for their next belly dancing class. Benjamin was gone for the next couple of days, visiting the Ridgefield bird sanctuary. He had offered to drive back that night, but India urged him to take his time. He and India had been together nearly every waking moment since that first night. She needed to be alone. She did not understand how he could stand to be with her so much. He never appeared annoyed with her—or tired of her. It was almost unnatural. They made love and talked for hours. Together they read, watched old movies, and studied the swans.

India had started taking notes, too, when they observed the swans. At the end of each day, they compared notes. Yesterday, his had read:

"32 swans total, 9 juvenile feeding at east end

"2 great blue heron

"1 red-tailed hawk

"The swans seemed to be accustomed to our presence."

India's journal had read, "23 adults, 9 juveys floated, ate, stroked one another. Bugged a great blue heron, and she cranked at us. The swans have not flown in days. Rhonda is right: there are advantages to being invisible. Too much goose shit everywhere."

Sometimes she and Benjamin just sat silently together. She sent him home to the garage every night. And when he left her alone she had an almost uncontrollable urge to call Jack. But she didn't. It wasn't fair to him. She sighed and looked out the window.

Benjamin wasn't with her right now and she did not want to constantly think about him.

Where was Rhonda?

Rhonda knocked as she opened India's front door.

"It smells like sex in here," Rhonda said as she walked inside.

"It most certainly does not!" India said.

"Really, it does," Rhonda said. "You should air the place out. How is our Mr. Swan?"

"Are you driving or what?" India asked, grabbing her purse.

"Yes."

"Then let's go."

They drove in silence for several minutes.

"I'm sorry I sounded so cranky," India said. "How are you doing?"

"We're fine," Rhonda said. "Just peachy."

"Do you like being a 'we'?" India asked. "Does it ever bother you that when someone thinks of one of you they automatically think of the other?"

"No! I figure I'm in good company," Rhonda said.

"Don't you worry about disappearing?"

Rhonda laughed. "Honey, I do not go into this world unnoticed."

"That's a fact," India said.

"So your sweetheart is gone and you miss him," Rhonda said.

"Yes, and it is very annoying! I don't like this feeling."

"Yes, you do."

"No, I don't, Rhonda."

"Well, get over it or cut him loose. Those are your choices. Beth called and told me what Daniel said about the class action suit. Do you think we should go ahead and try and get the money?"

India shrugged. Rhonda slowed the car as they neared town. "I'm not sure. We're going to brainstorm tomorrow at the POOL meeting."

"That'll be more like a brain flurry," Rhonda said.

India laughed.

Inside the Recreation Center, Violet warmed up with Cheryl, Ivy, Gina, and Clementine. India and Rhonda joined the line of women. Clementine patted India's butt as she went by, and India winked at her.

"OK, ladies, let's stretch those hands to the ceiling! Gracefully. Remember, you are dancers!"

They practiced creating figure eights with their hips, then their shoulders. Practiced walking in rhythm, performing figure eights, and dropping their hips. Violet tried to teach them the beginnings of the actual belly dance. She stood before them and moved her body like a snake. Her belly rippled, danced, undulated.

The women attempted to emulate her. Ivy was a natural, although she had little belly to ripple. Clementine was good, too.

"It's the same motion you make when you're—you know—making love," Violet said, demonstrating with her snake body. "Yes, India, that's right. You've got it now."

"India just needed the context," Rhonda said.

India laughed, broke away from the line, and danced around the women, attempting to make her Renaissance belly dance. Violet turned up the music, and they all broke ranks and danced. At first they tried to stay in belly dance mode. Soon they were making figure eights and circles and snakes with their hands, hips, shoulders, spine, all over the cafeteria, their bodies moving naturally to the sensual beat. After a few minutes they formed a line that snaked around the tables and chairs until they and the tape finished at the same time at the back of the room. They grabbed hands and bowed to one another.

"See you next week, ladies," Violet said as they let go of each other's hands.

"The POOLers are meeting tomorrow night at India's at six to figure out how we can raise money to screw the county," Rhonda said. "You're all welcome." She looked at India. "Right?"

"Sure," India said. "Eat before you come."

"India will make us something," Rhonda said.

"Don't count on it," India said.

"Good evening, dancers." A man's voice.

They turned to the entrance. Jack. India glanced at Violet. She smiled broadly. India looked back at the door. Jack wasn't looking at Violet; he was looking at India. He smiled.

India walked over to him. "What are you doing here?" she asked.

"I saw your car," he said. "So I thought I'd see if you wanted that cup of coffee."

India glanced over at Violet. She was putting her things into a bag.

India turned to Jack. "Why not? Rhonda drove, so if you can get me home later."

"Sure," he said.

Kim Antieau

Rhonda walked up to them. "Hello, Jack. Any word on Aviary Lumber?"

"Everything seems to check out," Jack said.

"He knows how much Turtle Pond means to me," India said. "He wouldn't let any harm come to it, would you, Jack?"

"Certainly not."

"Jack's going to take me home," India said.

Rhonda raised an eyebrow, then said, "All right. I'll talk to you later. Night." She walked away.

Jack and India went out into an icy cold night. Jack nervously opened his car door. India slid inside. Jack got in next to her.

They looked at each other and then laughed.

"Geez," India said. "I'm just coming over to your house. Why are we acting so weird?"

Jack started the car. "Yeah, I don't know why. It does feel kind of strange."

They drove silently to Jack's house. Once inside, Jack took her coat. Then she followed him into the kitchen. She sat at the table while he filled the kettle with water.

"So how have you been?" India asked as he put the pot on the stove. She glanced around. The place seemed the same.

"Good," he said. He got two cups and a jar of coffee from the cupboard and brought them to the table. He shook some coffee granules into one cup. He left the other empty.

India smiled. After all these years he finally remembered she liked her water hot—and clear. No coffee. No tea.

"We've been busy," he said. "How about you? They said you haven't even stopped at the library. Isn't that kind of strange?"

She shrugged. "I don't miss it at all. Is that hard for you to understand? You and I were always about our work, weren't we? Worked too long and too hard and got too tired to do anything but fall into bed with each other."

The kettle whistled. Jack went to the stove and got it. India watched as he steadily poured water into each cup. He set the kettle back on the stove, then sat next to India again.

"That's how you saw us? Too tired to turn to anyone else? Christ, India, that's cold."

"How did you see it?" India asked.

"Not like *that*," he said. "I really cared about you." He looked at her. "I still do."

They stared at one another. Jack slowly leaned toward her, and they kissed. India's stomach fluttered. How easy it would be to walk back into the bedroom with him. Make love. Just to see. Too see, if she could slip back into her old life.

"I miss you," Jack said quietly. Then he took a drink from his cup. "You really like Benjamin?" He didn't look at her.

"Yeah, I do."

"You don't know anything about him," Jack said.

"Let's not do this again," India said. She stood and went into the living room.

Jack followed. "But you don't know him."

"You are the one who recommended him to me," India said. "You were off running around with Violet. I trusted Benjamin because I trust you. So really it's your fault."

"I went out with Violet because I was sick of being rejected by you," Jack said. "I was trying to get a life, as you were always telling me. I didn't realize you would run off with the first man who offered."

"You never offered," India said. Her eyes widened. Where had that come from?

"I never offered?" Jack said. "You always said you just wanted things nice and easy. So things between us were nice and easy. If I'd known you wanted mystery and quick passionate sex, I would have obliged."

"Who says it's quick?" India snapped.

Jack came and put his arm across her shoulder. They sat on the couch together. She leaned against him. If she asked, she knew Jack would make love with her. She glanced at him. Should she ask? She sighed. What was she doing?

"I'm sorry," India said. "I didn't mean to yell at you. Sometimes you make me so mad."

"The feeling is mutual," Jack said.

She had spent many nights on this couch with Jack, watching movies and cuddling.

"Do you want to stay?" Jack whispered, taking her hand in his. "Everything Benjamin learned he learned from me."

India looked up at him. She could stay with him for the night. Then she could decide: old or new, familiar or unfamiliar.

No.

Jack grinned. India laughed. She kissed his cheek.

"I shouldn't have come," she said. "I'm going to go home and get some sleep."

She stood.

"You're always welcome here," Jack said.

"Thanks. Now take me home."

They drove in silence again. He stopped the car at her front door.

"There's more going on than you realize," Jack said. "Watch yourself."

"Jack, if you know something I need to know, just tell me," India said. "Otherwise..."

Jack shook his head. "There's just a lot happening."

"With Benjamin? Is there something I need to know about Benjamin?" She looked at Jack. Darkness pulsed between them.

Finally Jack said, "No, Benjamin's a good guy. It's just that it's hard for me. I love you, India."

Why was he saying this now? "You don't mean that."

Jack laughed. "That wasn't exactly the response I was hoping for," he said.

"I don't know what to say," India said.

"Don't say anything," Jack said. "I'll talk to you later."

India got out of the car. She watched Jack drive away. She unlocked her front door and stepped inside. What had just happened?

She had almost stayed with Jack, had almost had sex with him. That's what had happened. And now he said he loved her.

"Great timing, Jack."

She started to shut the door when she heard, "Knock, knock."

She opened the door wider.

"Benjamin!"

He looked sheepish.

"I thought you were staying another day," India said.

Benjamin shrugged. "It was only an hour and a half away. And I'd run out of batteries. And paper. Pencil. Food. Shelter." He leaned down to her ear. "And I missed you."

India smiled and said, "You are welcome. Come on in."

BENJAMIN STAYED THE night with India. He fell to sleep on her shoulder with her arms around him. India knew she would never get to sleep this way. She did not like being touched when she slept—could not imagine actually falling asleep in this position.

But she closed her eyes.

She dreamed a knight chased her through the woods. He rode a horse and carried a lance. Or was it something else? He held it out toward her as the horse's hooves thundered across the meadow. She screamed.

The dream startled her awake. Benjamin had moved away from her to the other side of the bed. She sat up.

Benjamin shifted, turned to her, and murmured. "Are

you all right?"

"Just a dream," she said.

"Do you want to talk about it?"

"No. Go to sleep."

"All right. Love you. See you in the morning."

She stared at his sleeping back.

Now, it seemed, the Swan Knight loved her.

She lay back down again. She slipped her hands under the covers and the elastic in Benjamin's underwear and rested her fingers on his hip; then she fell to sleep.

THE NEXT DAY, Benjamin left before the POOLers arrived. Clementine came with Marian and Nancy. Beth and Rhonda wandered in together. Beth told the group about their meeting with Daniel Salmonson.

"Where would we get that kind of money?" Nancy asked.

"We need something quick and easy," Marian said, "and positive. Good for the community."

"I suggested a bake sale," Clementine said. "A really expensive bake sale."

"That's the thing," India said. "Do we do lots of little fund raisers or one really big one?"

"Let's rob a bank and get it over with," Nancy said.

"Don't do the crime if you can't do the time," Marian said.

"I thought maybe we could get something published and sell that," India suggested, "but it takes so long."

"With the holiday coming, we won't be able to get much done anyway," Marian said.

"A holiday bazaar?" Rhonda offered.

"It's a little late to organize something like that," Beth said. "Excuse me." She got up and went to the bathroom.

"Don't you have any food, India?" Rhonda asked.

"I'm hungry, too," Marian said.

They both went into the kitchen.

"Well, I finished my holiday shopping today," Nancy said. "Deborah is the only one I shop for."

"What'd you get her?" Clementine asked.

"A dildo."

India laughed. "That was on her list to Santa?"

"A dildo?" Rhonda came back to the table.

"I thought she said a pilldough," Marian said.

"What the hell is a pilldough?" Nancy asked.

"I don't know. I thought that's what you said!"

"I've never used a dildo," Rhonda said. "'fraid I'd get electrocuted."

"Explain something to me," Clementine said. "Why would a lesbian use a dildo? Isn't that like saying you want a man? Isn't a dildo a mechanical penis? I thought the whole idea of having a woman was to get away from those things."

"Using a dildo doesn't mean we're really longing for men," Nancy said.

"Didn't you ever hear that old joke," Marian said. "What's the difference between a prick and a penis? A penis is hard and feels good going in and a prick is what it's attached to."

They all looked at her. She shrugged. "I remember

jokes."

"But you thought I said *pilldough*!" Nancy said.

Beth walked into the room. "What's a pilldough?"

The women laughed.

"Our two hours are up," Rhonda said. "We better get going."

"It's full moon tonight," Nancy said.

"Let's go out to the meadow and look at the moon," India suggested. "I've always wanted to do that but was too chicken to go out alone."

"All right," Marian said. "We can be like forest nymphs of old dancing under the full moon."

They began putting on their coats, hats, and scarfs.

"I think they called those nymphs witches and burned them at the stake," Beth said.

"Gee, those were the days," Marian said.

"Haven't you heard that round?" Nancy asked. "Something like, 'we are the witches back from the dead.' Something, something, something."

"We'll have to be quiet near the swans," India said.

They went outside into the December night. It seemed more like October. India pointed to the moon. It spilled silver over the meadow. The women linked arms and walked slowly so that the older women could keep up. Coyotes yipped in the distance.

"This is spooky," Marian said.

"It's beautiful," Clementine whispered.

"I could read in this light," Beth said.

"Yes, but it's so different from sunlight," India said, "even though it is sunlight. I can almost hear the fairies dancing."

They whispered to one another and went south of the cottonwood so they would not disturb the swans.

"It sounds like they're cooing to one another," Marian said.

They walked around the gate and out into the open meadow. The women tilted their heads. India closed her eyes and felt the moonlight on her face, could see it on her eyelids.

A coyote howled.

"Lions, tigers, and bears, oh my," Nancy whispered.

India grinned. She looked at her friends. She planted her feet apart on the ground. Her body tingled. She felt suddenly ancient, as if she had done this a million times before—stood with friends to protect what needed protecting. Stood with friends and danced under the moonlight.

"Some people believe moonlight can cure anything," Beth said. "Or cause anything. Like lunacy."

Several coyotes yipped together.

India opened her mouth and howled.

Then she said, "Beth, I hope this doesn't offend you but I'm taking my top off."

"You'll freeze," Beth said.

India took off her coat.

Nancy said, "What the hell," and began unbuttoning her jacket.

"I'm ready," Rhonda said.

Soon everyone but Beth was taking off their coats. Then they stopped and watched India. She pulled her shirt and camisole off at the same time.

And stood in the moonlight bare-breasted.

"It's cold!" she howled.

The others followed her example. Soon they all stood shirtless except for Beth.

"I can feel the moonlight just fine through all of my clothes," she said.

The partially bare-naked women howled at the moon, yipped like the coyotes, and danced in a circle with their breasts to the outside, shaking them, exposing them to moonlight. Beth clapped along with them.

"In defense of Mother Earth!" India called.

"Yes!" All of their hands shot up into the air.

Then they screamed and giggled and grabbed their clothes. India watched the women, saw their nakedness, and knew she looked like them. They were not invisible to her.

"You are beautiful, you natural women," India said.

"And cold. Let's go!" Nancy said.

They got dressed, then hurried back to the road and India's house. India kissed her friends goodbye. Then she sat at the table and waited for Benjamin. Soon after everyone had left, he returned.

As he took off his coat, he said, "I wasn't spying, I promise. I was taking a walk, and I saw all of you. I thought the others might be embarrassed, so I turned and hurried away."

"You saw us dancing naked in the moonlight?" India asked.

He sat next to her. "Yes. And it was one of the most

beautiful sights I've ever seen."

India laughed. "It was glorious!"

"It was so beautiful," Benjamin said. "I wished I'd had my camera. Not that I would have taken a picture without your permission. It was as if I had stumbled across the Swan Maidens cavorting here on Earth."

"That would have been quite a picture," India said. "We could have sold that to raise money."

She stared at Benjamin. Then she laughed.

"That's it. That's it. That's it! We'll sell pictures of us naked."

"What?"

India got up and began pacing. "I remember hearing about this group of older ladies in England who made calendars with pictures of themselves nude. It was for charity. And the Salt Island women up in British Columbia did it, too. The photographs were all very tasteful. You couldn't really see anything but skin. I saw the British calendar somewhere. Anna. I think someone got her one. One woman was painting so the easel was in front to her. Another pouring tea. All older women. The POOLers could do that, too. Only it wouldn't be a January to December calendar. It would be a true moon-thly calendar. A lunar calendar."

Benjamin laughed. "You think your friends are going to let anyone take pictures of them nude and then put it on a calendar to sell?"

"Those women in England and Canada are all very respectable women," India said. "Whatever that means, granted. But they felt good about what they did. One

Salt Island woman said she'd do just about anything to save the land, including taking off her clothes. I feel the same way. Printing a calendar wouldn't cost that much. I remember when I was doing some publicity for *Nature Girl* I found an ecologically safe printer in Portland to do my bookmarks. Polly at Ecology Printing. I bet printing would be two or three dollars a piece. We'd sell them for twenty bucks. That's eighteen dollars profit. If we sold six hundred, we'd have our $10,000."

"And who would you get to take these photographs?"

India looked at him.

"Oh no, not me."

"You've already seen them half-naked. They know and like you."

"I've already been accused of being a pornographer. I don't want to go through that again.

"This wouldn't be pornography. It's art!"

"It's selling your body to make money," Benjamin said. "That's what people will say."

"I don't care. What I say is we're beautiful women. We're not ashamed of who we are. Society thinks of us as invisible, as worthless, as sexless. Well, we'll make sure we're seen. And if people want to support our cause they can buy the calendars."

"I agree you're all beautiful but—"

"Benjamin, I know you understand what it's like to be tossed to the side, to feel like all you've accomplished is meaningless. Think how wonderful it would be for these women to see themselves again, really, as respected and

156   *Kim Antieau*

valued."

"They'd essentially be taking their clothes off in front of thousands of strangers."

"I want to make this place safe for all of us," India said, "the people, the swans, turtles. Apparently I need $10,000 to start that process. I have tried reasoning with these people. I have tried laying out the scientific facts. They don't believe anything we say—and you know why? Because they see us as old women who have no power or value. I know that's difficult to believe, but you haven't been through this struggle with us."

Benjamin was silent. He shrugged. "I'm sure the calendars would sell, but I'm not sure I want to be the one taking the photos. This is going to be a big deal, India. If I'm the photographer, they'll bring up my past. I'll have to go through all that again, plus your project might be tainted because of my involvement."

"It's not *your* past," India said. "You didn't do anything wrong. We wouldn't be doing anything wrong here either. But before we make any decisions I need to talk to our lawyer and the POOLers to see if they'll actually do it."

India kissed Benjamin on the lips and sat next to him. She wanted him to do this with her; she knew it was the right thing to do. It would work. She knew it would be joyous. Wonderful. And awful. Benjamin said he wanted her to see him. She wanted to. She knew she had often seen Raymond as someone to do what she wanted done. Was she like that with everyone? She saw a way, like now, and she was certain about it and didn't understand why everyone didn't fall into step with her.

"Think about doing the pictures for this project," India said, "but I don't want you to do anything that will hurt you."

"I want to make you happy."

"It is not your responsibility to make me happy, Benjamin," she said.

"It is intriguing," Benjamin said. "To make pictures of these women. It could be inspiring."

"And fun," India said. "It's about time the world saw some old broads running around naked."

CHAPTER ELEVEN

BENJAMIN WAS GONE when India awakened. He left a note on the kitchen table: "Swanning. Love, B."

India smiled and opened the curtains. She breathed deeply when she saw the wild swans floating on the pond. She knew the swans would eventually leave, but every morning when she saw they had survived the night, she felt as though the Earth could keep spinning one more day.

She ate breakfast. Then she started to call Jack but instead phoned Daniel Salmonson. She told him her plan.

He was silent for so long India finally said, "Daniel, are you there?"

"Yes, I'm here. Well, India, I think you could get the money making the lunar calendar, and I admire your ingenuity."

"Daniel! Speak!"

"There could be a lot of fuss, Indy. It's a small town. It could backfire and spoil the jury pool for the class action suit. You could lose all credibility and never be able to get a judgment."

"We don't have any credibility with any of the people in power now. I think we will get a lot of press. I'll make certain we do. And every time anyone asks why we're doing it, we'll tell them: because we believe the county is poisoning us."

"Careful about the hyperbole. We don't want a libel suit."

"It's a fact they sprayed Marlo's property, and she got sick. It's a fact they are using pesticides that—"

"I'm just saying when you speak to the press, be careful what you say. It can be used in the lawsuit," Daniel said. "Stick to the facts."

"So you're not advising against this?" India said.

"I'm certainly not advising you to do it," Daniel said. "I don't know what the repercussions will be. But you're right, they aren't listening now. I know Andrew and the commissioners. Their biggest fear is bad publicity. Or any publicity, really."

"Good," India said.

"Have you gotten anyone to agree to do this yet?"

"You mean strip naked for the camera? No. I'm going to try and get the POOLers together today."

"Good luck," Daniel said. "I looked into Aviary Lumber. They seem legitimate. The CEO recently stepped down and was replaced by his son, but they've always utilized ecologically sound methods in the woods. No clear-cutting. No old growth harvests."

"That's a relief," India said.

"Let me know what the POOLers say about the calendar," Daniel said.

It took two hours of phone calls to settle on a time and place for an emergency POOL meeting. India's house, 5:15.

"No, I don't want to tell you what it's about right now," she told each one. "I want to talk with everyone at once."

She called Anna, asked her to attend the meeting and to bring the calendar of the naked English ladies.

"The calendar? That was last year, wasn't it? I'm not sure I have it."

Anna, who owned the bakery, had never seen a piece of paper she would throw out. Her house was filled with old magazines, newspaper clippings, and books.

"Anna, I know you save old calendars," India said. "You showed me a ten year old cat calendar a couple of months ago."

"All right," Anna said. "I'll see what I can find."

"I'll feed you," India said. "Soup."

"I'll bring the bread," Anna said.

"And the calendar," India said.

Benjamin came in as she hung up from the last call.

"Hi! I'm so glad to see you," she said. "I've been on the phone forever. But the POOLers are coming over tonight."

Benjamin nodded and slipped off his coat. India went to him and kissed him. He held her against him for a moment.

"You want to help me make the Soup to Seduce?" India asked.

"You don't have to seduce me," Benjamin said, looking down at her and grinning. "I'm willing and able."

India playfully pushed him away.

"Not you," India said, going into the kitchen. "I'm hoping the POOLers will be so sated with food they'll agree to anything."

"Sure, I'll help," Benjamin said. "It's raining out anyway."

"What a wimp," she said. "You can't stand a little rain? What kind of Pacific Northwesterner are you?"

He pulled up her shirt a couple of inches and put his hands on her bare skin. She cried out and jumped away.

"OK. Cold and rainy. You stay here with me," she said. "You'll find yellow split peas in the cupboard. Rinse three cups of them in a colander, please. Then put them in a big soup pot with water."

India placed two turnips, three carrots, three stalks of celery, four potatoes, an onion, and several cloves of garlic on the counter.

"This is seduction soup?" Benjamin asked as they rinsed the vegetable.

"I figure they'll be so sleepy from all the carbs they'll agree to anything," India said.

"You want these onions minced?"

"No. Peel what needs to be peeled and cut into a few

pieces, then throw it all into the pot. Then I just let it cook for a few hours. How were the swans today?"

"Good. I only counted one pink billed juvey swan today. There were two before. I'm not sure how fast the bill turns to black, but I doubt it would happen overnight."

"How many grays total?"

"Nine," Benjamin said. He peeled the onion, cut it into four pieces, and then dropped the pieces into the soup pot.

"I watched India Jr. today. Her neck and head are still gray. She was off by herself. Every once in a while one of the white swans would join her."

"She's probably an obnoxious teenager and her parents are trying to get her to come home at a decent hour," India said.

Benjamin laughed.

India cut the carrot into the three pieces and the potatoes into six, and slid them into the soup.

"Now we let it cook," India said. "I was thinking about the swan book, the one you talked about us doing, and I think we should do it, if you're still interested. It could be a coffee table book. I would write the text, but it wouldn't be long, maybe a retelling of the Swan Maiden story, I'm not sure. The text could run at the bottom of the photos. It might be fun."

The soup began to boil. India watched it. Benjamin leaned against the refrigerator, his arms crossed.

"Would you have time to do that if you're also busy with the calendar?" Benjamin asked.

"Sure. You'll be doing all the work. On the swan

book, I mean."

Benjamin smiled. "OK. I'll start taking photos, and then we can go through and look at the new and old ones.

She skimmed the foam off of the roiling soup, turned down the burner, and covered the pot.

"Benjamin, I feel like since last night, since I asked you to take the photos, something has been different between us. I don't want there to be. I don't care if you take the photos or not. I know a woman in Underwood. A photographer. A woman might be better anyway."

Benjamin opened his arms. India went into them, and they embraced. He kissed the top of her head.

"I don't want you to be disappointed in me," Benjamin said.

"I'm not," India said. "I want you to do what's best for you." She squeezed him and looked up into his face. "Actually I want you to do what's best for me, but I'm trying to be a better partner."

Benjamin smiled. "Partners. I like that."

They let each other go, went into the living room, and sat on the couch.

"I got a letter yesterday," Benjamin said, "that got me thinking. The principal of the school where I used to teach wants me back for six weeks while one of his teachers is out. I'd be teaching the same classes as before."

"When?" India asked. She felt slightly sick to her stomach.

"February."

"Are you going to do it?" she asked.

"At first I wanted to rip the letter up, but I need to make a living. It's what I've been trained to do. I just don't know if I can trust any of them again. I know intellectually only one student accused me, but there could be another waiting in the wings."

"That's true," India said.

"It's nice being here and doing this," Benjamin said. "But my money will run out soon."

"Maybe you could get a teaching job here," India said.

"Do you want me to stay then?"

"Yes!" Yes, yes, yes, yes!

"I dread that process, too, looking for a job. I'll have to tell them what happened."

"No, you don't, Benjamin. You act like a guilty man. They *accused* you. You didn't do anything."

"I know, I know. But like you said about women getting older and becoming invisible, after a while you start believing what they say yourself."

"When do you have to let him know?" India asked.

"Sometime in the next couple of weeks," Benjamin said.

India put her head on his shoulder. "Well, the swans will probably be gone by February."

"Yes," Benjamin said. "I thought of that."

"We could probably finish our book by then," India said.

Benjamin laughed. "Yes, let's be practical. What about us being separated for six weeks?"

India sat up.

"India," Benjamin said. "I love you. I don't want to leave you."

India stared out the window. She loved him, too. She did. Right now it was making her sick to her stomach thinking of him gone. She didn't like this feeling. What was this feeling? Dependence? Did love equal dependence? She wouldn't be destroyed if he left now. She knew that. What if they were together for ten years and he left—or died? What would happen to her then?

"India?"

"Can we talk about this later?" she asked.

"Sure."

She lay down and put her head in his lap.

"I want to strategize tonight's meeting," she said. "You know, be focused on that."

Benjamin stroked her hair.

"Look on the bright side," India said. "Maybe we'll hate each other by February."

ANNA WAS THE last to arrive for the POOL meeting. The other women ate salad and the golden split pea soup.

India pulled Anna into her office. "Can I see the calendar?"

"Sure. Here." She pulled it out from her bag. "I'll go take the bread out."

India flipped through the calendar. It was as she had remembered: tasteful beautiful photographic portraits of the women engaged in activities with various items strategically placed to block the camera's view of their total naked selves.

India returned to the POOLers. She set the calendar at the end of the kitchen counter where someone might see it. She glanced around the kitchen and living room and counted: Cheryl, Gina, Clementine, Nancy, Marian, Beth, Rhonda, Anna. Nine including her.

She got herself a bowl of soup, then sat on the floor.

"This bread is great, Anna," Rhonda said. "You are magic."

The other women agreed.

"What about my soup?" India asked. "What am I? Chopped liver?"

"The soup is great, too," Marian said. "I told you earlier."

"Oh yeah, thanks." India smiled. She was nervous. Her natural reaction to that feeling was hostility. She should not be hostile.

Be congenial, she told herself. Be nice.

Nancy reached across the counter from her place on the stool and slid the calendar toward her. She opened it and flipped through the pages. She read the back cover, then looked at India. She smiled and shook a finger at her.

Nancy had figured it out.

No screaming yet.

"Whatcha got?" Marian asked Nancy.

Marian opened the calendar.

"Oh, a nudey calendar. Is this another present for Deborah?"

"No, Marian, it's an old calendar."

"Oh." She turned to the next month. "Hmmm. These

are quite nice. Wouldn't it be something to have the confidence to do a thing like this?"

Cheryl and Rhonda looked over Marian's shoulder as she turned the pages.

"Too bad someone didn't have a camera last night," Rhonda said. "We too could be stars."

"They did this calendar to raise money for charity," Anna said. "India asked me to bring it here tonight to show you all."

Rhonda turned to India, an eyebrow raised. She put her hands on her hips. "Oh?"

"What was it you wanted to talk to us about?" Clementine asked.

India stood and cleared her throat.

"I think I've figured out a way we can raise money for the lawyer."

All eyes were on her.

"By doing this?" Rhonda asked, holding up the calendar. "Are you out of your mind?

"Doing what?" Clementine got up and took the calendar from Rhonda. Beth, Gina, and Clementine looked at the naked English ladies together.

"I called an eco-printer in Portland," India said. "They can do it for $2.00 a calendar. If we charged $20 per calendar and sold one thousand, we'd net $18,000. We can pay the lawyer plus have some money left over to fund other programs. As you can see, the photographs are very tasteful. We can find a photographer we trust. We could retain all rights to the photographs. It would be our project. Right now the county sees us as nothing.

We have no power, they believe. We need the money to get some power. These women became celebrities. They were proud of themselves. We should be proud of ourselves."

"We are," Marian said. "What's that got to do with taking off our clothes?"

"Because that's what will sell the calendars," Cheryl said.

"Plus we could play on the idea of being au naturel," Nancy said. "We're trying to protect nature. We are natural women."

"I like that," Anna said.

"I'm not sure the town is ready to see the postmaster, librarian, baker, and restaurateur naked," Gina said.

"I figured that instead of doing a regular calendar, since the British ladies already do that, we could do a monthly lunar calendar complete with the phases of the moon."

"I like that," Nancy said.

"We could be Nature Women," Marian said, "like India's book."

"Or Natural Women," Anna said, "like Nancy said."

"Well," Beth said.

The room fell silent. The women looked at Beth. India clenched her fists behind her back.

"I was in town today," Beth said, "at the commissioners' meeting. I tried to talk to them about the issue of pesticide spraying. Dick Lament said that I had had my three minutes, and they weren't going to listen to me any longer. And they didn't. They just kept going on with their business as if I weren't even in that room." She breathed deeply. "So I say, let's try it. We get final say on what pictures are used and how it's distributed. I do have some practical questions. If it's a lunar calendar, doesn't that usually start at new moon?"

"That's in two weeks," Nancy said, "since last night was full."

"That's not much time," Gina said.

"Ideally we should have thought of this a year ago," India said. "But now is all we have. I've put together newsletters and magazines. I know what to do. I've talked to the printer; she'll print the calendars as soon as we bring it to her. She really liked the idea. Recycled paper, soybean-based inks. If we haul ass, we could get this ready for the stores before Christmas."

"None of these English women are big," Rhonda said. "Some of us are fat."

"So?" India said.

"Easy for you to say," Rhonda said.

"The better to see you, my dear," India said.

Rhonda made a noise.

"I woke up in the middle of the night last night," India said, "thinking about all of this. Thinking about image. When I was a teenager I had really bad skin. I mean awful. Whiteheads covered my face. They went away eventually and a couple of years later, I was rummaging through a drawer and came across this 5 x 7 school picture of me from two years earlier. And there was my grotesque face for all to see. I started sobbing and asked my mom how she could have let me out of the house.

She said I wasn't ugly because I hadn't seen myself as ugly. So no one else had. She was right. No one had ever made fun of me. No one had ever said a word to me. Lately I've been feeling insignificant, and I'm tired of it. Rhonda, you've taught me more about being my own person than almost anyone I know by example. I want to do this calendar, but I don't want anyone else to do this under pressure. If we do it, we have to understand shit will hit the fan."

"Speaking of fans, will we have a wind machine to make our hair look cool?" Nancy asked, grinning.

"What little hair we have left," Gina said.

"Who will take the pictures?" Anna asked.

"Whoever we want," India said.

"Did you ask Benjamin Swan?" Rhonda asked.

"Benjamin is a photographer?" Clementine asked.

"Actually I was having a conversation with him when I came up with this idea. Last night we had a POOL meeting and afterward several of us went outside and danced in the moonlight without our shirts on."

"That must have been a little nippy in the tippy," Gina said.

"Benjamin saw us," India said.

Nancy laughed. Marian covered her face with her hands.

"He was out walking and there we were," India said. "He didn't stay and watch. He turned around and went the other way, but he did tell me it was a beautiful sight to stumble upon."

"Well, there you go," Rhonda said. "He's already seen

some of us naked. Ask him to do it."

"I did."

"And?" Rhonda asked.

"He has some reservations."

"About seeing thirteen bare-naked old ladies?" Nancy asked. "I don't blame him."

"No, it's nothing like that."

"Let's vote on whether or not we want to do the calendar," Beth said. "All in favor of creating a calendar with us as the naked subjects as a fund raiser for POOL raise your right hands."

One by one, all the women raised their hands.

"All right!" India said. "Now, we need someone to coordinate publicity, someone to talk with bookstores and other outlets, someone who'll be in charge of mail orders, and we need some more old broads. I volunteer to write the copy and work with the printer. Anyone want to actually do the calendar part of the calendar?"

Nancy said, "I'm sure Deborah will do this with us, and she's a publicist. We'll do the publicity, write the press releases, stuff like that. Do we want to spread the word further than Portland and Vancouver?"

"Hey, if we're going to do it, let's do it," Rhonda said. "Eugene, Hood River, Seattle. The whole Pacific Northwest."

"I've still got some ins with booksellers and other retailers," Anna said. "Anyone want to help me with that?"

Gina raised her hand.

"Violet does astrology," Clementine said. "I heard her

and Ivy talking about it. She could help do that part of the calendar. I could work on that with her."

"What's our criteria for more old broads?" Nancy asked.

"Over forty," Rhonda said.

"Forty is pretty young," Gina said. "How about forty-five? Does that knock any of us out?"

"Deborah is right on the cusp," Nancy said.

"Cradle-robber," India said.

"You should talk," Nancy said.

"OK, over forty-four," Gina said.

India heard a knock on the door through the din of voices. She went to see who it was.

"Benjamin."

"Can I talk with you?"

"Now?"

He nodded. She grabbed her coat and stepped outside, closing the door behind her. She put on her coat.

"Did they say yes?" he asked.

"They did," India said, grinning.

"I'll do it," Benjamin said. "I'll take the pictures. It'll be good. I am acting like a guilty man, and I haven't done anything wrong. I want to do it, but I want the women to decide if they want me after I've told them what happened at Mott."

"You don't have to do this, Benjamin," India said.

"I know."

"Will you do it for free?" India asked.

"What?"

"Will you donate your services?"

Benjamin laughed. "Yes, I will."

"OK. Let's go talk to them."

Benjamin nodded.

"What changed your mind, anyway?" India asked.

"You did. If you're brave enough to take off your clothes, I should be brave enough to take pictures of it."

India laughed. She punched him lightly in the stomach.

"I'm glad I can be so inspiring," India said. She opened the front door, and they stepped inside.

"Ladies," India called, "Benjamin would like to talk with you. Do you all know Benjamin Swan?"

The women turned to them.

"Yeah, we all know him," Clementine said. "What's up? You gonna take naked pictures of us or what?"

"I would like to, but I wanted to tell you something first," he said. "I used to be a teacher at Mott. Last year a young girl accused me of taking pornographic pictures of her and having sex with her. I was innocent. She eventually admitted she lied and that her boyfriend had taken the photos. But it was all over the newspapers. India's told me about what you've all been trying to accomplish, and I'm behind you all the way."

"I read about that thing at Mott," Rhonda said. "You should have sued their asses."

"I remember it, too," Gina said. "They done you wrong big time."

"You were *accused* of taking naked pictures," Nancy said. "We want you to *actually* take the pictures. You think you can handle that?"

"I don't think it'll be a problem," Benjamin said.

"Then I say let's hire the accused pervert and get on with it," Nancy said.

"I agree," Anna said. "What are we paying him?"

"He's volunteering," India said, "like all of you are. And we need to get started right away. Do you have the equipment you need?"

"I only need my camera for now," Benjamin said.

"We never did figure out what to call this calendar," Rhonda said.

"Bare naked ladies," Marian said.

"Nature women," Beth said.

"Natural women," Nancy offered.

"Something along the nature lines," Clementine said.

"When can you start?" India asked Benjamin.

"Ideally, with the Nature theme, we would want to shoot outdoors, but it's too cold. Instead, why don't each of you find a place at home or at work where you feel comfortable doing what you love."

"I don't want a lot of people watching this," Rhonda said.

"No one has to be there but me and my assistant," Benjamin said, "and that assistant could be India."

"We need to get this done this week," India said. "Can we do it?"

Benjamin nodded. "Let's work out a schedule right now."

By the end of the evening, they had a plan of action. Cheryl would be the first subject. She lived out in Home Valley near Marian, who would be second, then Clementine after lunch when the restaurant was closed.

After the women left, India and Benjamin sat at the kitchen table.

"What have I done?" India asked.

Benjamin laughed. "Started a revolution," he said.

"You want to go make out?" India asked.

"I have to save my strength," Benjamin said. "No sex until this is over."

India laughed. She got up, pushed the table back, and sat on Benjamin's lap. She kissed his mouth.

"I don't believe you."

"Good thing," he said. He picked her up and carried her into the bedroom.

CHAPTER TWELVE

IN THE MORNING, India and Benjamin ate a quick breakfast, watched the swans from afar for a few minutes, then headed to Home Valley in India's car.

"That's really all the equipment you need?" India wondered.

"Just my digital camera. We want it to be natural, right?"

She nodded. "I'm so nervous I feel like throwing up."

"I'm glad I'm not the only one," Benjamin said.

"You're supposed to be reassuring me," India said.

"Why?"

"Because you're the Swan Knight," India said.

"And you're our fearless leader."

"OK. OK. This is going to be great," India said. "It'll work out just fine."

"That's right."

At Home Valley, they turned up Berge Road. India had never been to Cheryl's house, only driven by on the way to Marian's. Now she turned up the long and windy road to a white ranch house next to a long gray barn-like building. Evergreens surrounded the property. A dog barked in the distance.

Cheryl came out and greeted them as they got out of the car.

"Charlie took the dog for a walk," Cheryl said, "so we could have some peace."

"What's he think about this?" India asked.

"He's looking forward to seeing the photos," she said.

India laughed. "Good."

"Let's go into here," Cheryl said, leading the way to the barn.

"It's beautiful here," India said.

"We enjoy it," she said. She opened the door, and they all stepped through it. They were inside housing that covered an Olympic-sized pool.

"Benjamin, you asked where I was most comfy," Cheryl said. "That's here. What now?"

"I'd like to talk with you for a few minutes," Benjamin said. "I'll be adjusting my camera. Checking out the light, things like that."

"All right." Cheryl smiled at India.

"But you go into town to swim with Rhonda," India

said. "Why do that when you have this?"

"For the company," she said, "and sometimes I have people over here, but mostly this is my solitary place. I can open these big doors—they're garage doors—and it's like being outdoors. Almost."

"Are these pictures of you?" Benjamin asked. He stood looking at several framed photographs on the wall next to a shelving unit partially filled with towels.

"Yes," Cheryl said. "I was on the Olympic swim team. An alternate. I loved swimming when I was a girl. Any pool, pond, even a few rivers. My father said I was part fish. Salmon, he said because my hair was red back then."

Benjamin looked through his finder as Cheryl spoke.

"Anyway, I was an alternate for the four hundred meter. As it happens, I fell in love with one of the swimmers I met along the way, and I got pregnant. This was before abortion was legal, and I didn't know how to find anyone to do an illegal abortion—probably a good thing given the stories I've heard. So I dropped out of the Olympics. Found a country boy back home to marry me. I miscarried the opening day of the Olympics. 1952 in Finland. I was so angry. I wished I had miscarried earlier. I was already married by that time. I was angry for years. Angry at Charlie."

"He was the country boy?" India asked.

"Yes. After our third child, I was so depressed I nearly drowned in my own sadness. Charlie went out every morning before work and every night after work building this. When he finally finished and brought me out here, I took off all of my clothes and dove right in. I felt like a salmon in that moment, realizing I had been swimming upstream all those years looking for home. When that warm water closed in around me, I felt like I had finally come home."

"Would you feel comfortable doing that now?" Benjamin asked.

"Oh yes. I swim in the buff all of the time, only usually not with company."

The sun came out from behind clouds and streamed in through the windows, creating slanted columns of gold. The water became robin egg blue.

"That is beautiful," Benjamin said. "Let's try to catch some of that light. If you can, pretend we aren't here."

"All right," Cheryl said.

She walked to the other end of the pool and took off her clothes and left them in a pile. She stood out of the sunlight. Then she climbed up and got onto the diving board. Slowly she walked out onto the end of it. A bit of sunlight touched her toes. She breathed deeply. India glanced at Benjamin. He was busily snapping pictures. She looked back at Cheryl. She appeared so serene and powerful.

Suddenly, Cheryl flew up into the air and then dove down, her body a perfect arrow as she went in to the clear water without a splash. India watched Cheryl underwater, flashing silver. Benjamin kept right in front of her at the other end of the pool, taking pictures, until Cheryl came part way out of the water—like India had seen fish do along the Columbia River as they leapt up to catch an evening insect. Water flowed from her, her white hair was plastered against her head, and she was a water nymph, part water, part woman. Then she was gone again.

"Beautiful," Benjamin said.

Cheryl's head popped up in the middle of the pond.

"Great!" Benjamin called. "That was amazing."

Cheryl swam to the side. Benjamin leaned over, and India could not hear what they said to one another. A few moments later, Cheryl got out of the pool and sat at the edge of it, in the sunlight, both legs up with her arms around them, her chin on her knees.

Benjamin took several close-up photos. India got a towel from one of the shelves and went over to Cheryl. The older woman took the towel, wrapped herself in it, and stood.

"Benjamin says that's all he needs," Cheryl said. "That was painless. Rather marvelous, actually. He showed me the pictures. Would you like to take a swim, India?"

India glanced at Benjamin. She couldn't really say no.

"OK."

Benjamin went to the other side of the room. India took off her clothes. Cheryl dropped her towel, and the two women jumped into the heated pool. India hadn't been skinny dipping in years. The water felt like ecstasy. India closed her eyes and let herself sink for a moment. Then she pushed herself to the surface.

"I'll race you," Cheryl called.

India laughed. "I bet you'll win."

MARIAN'S HOUSE WAS freezing. She let India use her daughter's blow dryer to get her hair dried. Marian made them hot tea. India's chill from the pool dissipated as they sat at Marian's kitchen table. Outside, the light was still golden. They had passed Marian's chestnut grazing in the front yard. Marian began unpinning her hair. India watched as she put one bobby pin down next to the other on the red and white checkered tablecloth. When all of the pins were out, she unwound her hair and brought the braid down over her right shoulder. The end of the braid reached her waist.

"I didn't know your hair was that long," India said.

Marian smiled. "Now you know why I agreed to this so easily."

"What did Katie say?" India asked.

"If she were thirteen I think she'd disown me," Marian said, "but she's nineteen now. Can you believe it? She's embarrassed, but she knows she'll survive it." She took the braid apart. "Benjamin, I know it's cold out, but my favorite place is atop Nutty out there."

"I'll take pictures as fast as I can," he said.

"She's traveled part of the Pacific Crest trail with me," Marian said. "We've been all over these woods. She's fought off cougars with me. Scared off coyotes. Eaten her fair share of garden vegetables along with the rabbits. When my hair was falling out from the chemo, she used to nibble on it. Really. It was the funniest thing. As if she were saying, 'Just shave it off, lady!' So I did. I shaved it all off and left it in a pile at her feet. Beauti-

Kim Antieau

ful brown hair. I hoped the birds took it and wove it into their nests. Later my hair grew back gray. And thick. I got Nutty the year Katie was born. I rode her when I was pregnant. Katie grew up running alongside her and up on her back. Now the vet wants to put her down. She's terminally ill, she says. Horses and dogs seem to know what to do to fix themselves when they're ill. What to eat. I figure Nutty might be on her way gone, but I'm not speeding it along. She stuck with me through my sickness. I'll stick by her with hers. She seems perfectly content. She's always bugging me to go for a ride. I thought today would be a good time to go. Maybe for the last time." She shrugged. "Maybe not."

Marian stood. Her wavy hair fell below her waist. Marian picked up a brown blanket from the back of her chair. The three of them went outside. Nutty whinnied.

"Here we are, girl," Marian said. She held out her hand and a carrot seemed to appear out of thin air. India looked at Benjamin. He smiled.

"You just keep doing what you're doing," Benjamin told them.

Marian put the blanket on Nutty's back. The horse nuzzled her. Marian took off her sweater, shirt, and bra, keeping her hair over her breasts, so that they were never actually bare.

"OK, Benjamin, turn away from us."

Benjamin did as he was asked. Marian took off her shoes, slacks, and underwear. She set her clothes in a neat pile on the ground.

"Can you give me a leg up?" Marian asked.

"Certainly." India bent over and locked her fingers together. Marian's sole pressed against her fingers, and she sprang onto Nutty's back. She adjusted her hair, then said, "OK, Benjamin."

Benjamin faced them again. India stepped away. Marian sat proudly on the horse. Nutty held her head up high. She did not look ill to India. The horse walked slowly toward the woods. Benjamin snapped pictures. He asked Marian to stop the horse a couple of times. Then he told her to go toward the woods. Steam rose from the edges of the evergreen forest, creating a kind of fairy tale mist. Maid Marian and her horse walked through the mist and into the forest as Benjamin took pictures of it all.

India smiled as she watched them. Maybe this would turn out after all.

BENJAMIN TOOK CLEMENTINE'S pictures in the kitchen of her restaurant while she chopped vegetables. The vegetables were spread out beautifully before her: broccoli, cauliflower, carrots, onions, eggplant. A vase of yellow and red flowers stood next to the wooden pepper mill and salt shaker. She chopped with a green tea towel thrown over her shoulder and falling down her front.

"I should have done this earlier," Clementine said. "Cooking naked. How liberating! We'll see what happens when people eat this soup tomorrow. Cooking is magic, you know. My customers might start running around bare-naked. Wouldn't that be a sight!"

"Have you always liked cooking?" India asked.

Clementine shook her head. "No. I started cooking

because I was miserable and depressed and couldn't imagine how I was going to keep on going. They'd just scraped out my female parts, the ones inside. I wasn't getting any younger. When I looked in the mirror I couldn't see myself. Nobody else could either. One day I sat down and started chopping vegetables—you know, to keep from chopping up myself or someone else. In the end I had all these bits of colorful vegetables and didn't know what to do with them, so I dropped them into the pot. Suicide Stew, I called it. It was so good I just giggled as I ate it. The next day I made another pot of soup. Clementine's Secret Clam Chowder. The secret is there are no clams. Next day another soup. I loved it. Those soups kept me going. Still do."

"I never knew that," India said.

"You never asked, honey," she said.

"I've got what I need," Benjamin said. "Thanks, Clementine."

"Check back tomorrow to see if everyone is running around naked," Clementine said.

AT HOME AGAIN, India and Benjamin ate leftover stir-fried vegetables and rice. Then they sat silently on the couch. India wondered how something so simple as talking to people and taking pictures could be so tiring. Benjamin had really been doing all the work. She leaned her head against his shoulder. The phone rang. Benjamin answered it.

"Hello, Beth. Sure I can take photos in the moonlight, but it'll be cold. Well, I don't mind but—OK. Let's try it."

Benjamin hung up the phone.

India laughed. "You can't dissuade Beth once she's decided on a thing."

"I guess not." Benjamin shook his head.

"So what is the thing?"

"There's a spot up near her place where the moonlight comes through the trees, and she wants her photo taken there. She said it'll be at the right spot in about an hour."

"Are you up for it?" India asked.

"Why not?"

"You're such a good sport," India said. "I watched you all day. You were really good with those women. You made them feel comfortable. You listened."

"It was a team effort, India Lake. You listened to them, too."

"They're amazing people," India said. "I should really pay more attention to them myself."

Benjamin and India parked at the end of Beth's long steep drive. She stood at her mailbox waiting. The moonlight was bright, the trees pillars of darkness.

"Where to?" India asked.

"Shhh," Beth said. "Listen."

A distant bird. Their breathing.

"Are your eyes adjusted?" Beth asked.

"Almost," Benjamin said.

Beth took India's arm. She led them down a leaf-strewn path toward the forest. Their feet kicked up leaves as they walked.

"You know, dear," Beth said. "I have never quite mastered relationships. After all these years, I relate better to all of this. This brings me joy. These woods. These places I have tramped through for the last thirty years. This makes sense to me: the turtles at the pond, the swans, the moon. These magnificent trees. See the bare top of that tree. That's old growth, dear. Right here, we have several old growth trees. I'm not sure how they survived, but they did."

The path turned. The world was clear and distinct in the moonlit darkness. Ahead, India saw several tall cedars. The moonlight lay in a silver pool in the midst of these cedars. The three people stopped.

"It's like a spotlight," India whispered.

"The other night," Beth said, "I didn't understand the need of the group to stand naked in the moonlight. Then I remembered this spot, and I wondered what it would be like. So, India, you come with me to hold my coat and robe. That's all I wore besides my boots! Benjamin, you figure where you need to be to take a good photograph."

India did as she was told. When she and Beth reached the moonlit center, Beth called, "Are you ready, Benjamin? I want to do this quickly."

"Yes," he answered. "Go ahead."

First she shed her coat, then her robe. India took the proffered clothes and stepped quickly out of the camera frame.

Beth stood in the shaft of moonlight. She tilted her head back and held her arms open. It was a pose of adoration. Supplication? Of *being*.

India's eyes teared up. She was certain she had never seen anything quite as beautiful as this seventy-some-thing woman standing naked under the full moon.

After a minute or so, Beth said, "OK?"

"OK," Benjamin agreed.

India hurried over to Beth and helped her on with her robe and coat.

"I forgot to take off my boots," Beth said.

"Don't worry about it," Benjamin said. "You were beautiful."

"Take me home now," Beth said. "I am drunk with moonlight."

INDIA SPOONED UP against Benjamin's back. He breathed deeply. She was glad he could fall to sleep so quickly after such an eventful day.

India whispered, "Good night, my love. You are a good man."

Then she fell to sleep, too.

CHAPTER THIRTEEN

BENJAMIN TOOK PICTURES of Gina in her greenhouse. She giggled as she took off her clothes and tossed them to India, who ran around the green house trying to catch them before they hit the ground. Gina surrounded herself with flowers and tall green ferns. She looked like a tiny dark-haired flower fairy. Laughing, she cut flowers from their stems and covered herself in flower circles of red, yellow, purple, and blue until it looked as though her body were blossoming—or as if she were the universe and multicolored suns were bursting into existence within her.

"George and I make love here all of the time," Gina said quietly to India as Benjamin took pictures. "Right there on that bench." She pointed to a bench along the greenhouse wall. "Now that I don't have to worry about getting pregnant, I can do it all of the time. Poor old, guy." She laughed. "It's great fun. Don't anyone tell you getting old ain't sexy."

India laughed.

"We even did it in the post office once," Gina said. "But I didn't like that. Here on the bench or warm in our bed. Those are my favorite places. Remember that when you're writing our bios." Gina looked toward the camera and smiled.

"Gina, it's not like a Playboy calendar," India said. "I'm not going to say where you all like doing it."

Gina looked at her. "Why not? You said you wanted to make us visible. What makes us more visible than letting the world know we still have sex lives. No matter how much the idea might revolt others."

India laughed.

ANNA WAS SURROUNDED by books and bread. Her lap and arms were filled with loaves of bread and sheaves of wheat and she looked like the Earth and grain goddess Ceres, ready to feed the world.

"Gina says I should talk about everyone's sex life in the biographical page," India said. "What do you think?"

Anna tried to remain very still for the camera.

"Hmmm," she said, barely moving her lips. "I think it would make for a short biography."

THEY WENT NEXT door to Freddy's house. Freddy didn't

come to many POOL meetings, but she supported their mission and readily agreed to pose when India phoned her. She met them downstairs in her workout room. When Benjamin said he was ready, Freddy took off her shirt and began hitting a punching bag dressed only in a pair of purple boxing shorts. Her body was taut and firm. Benjamin had to move quickly to keep up with the sixty-plus year old.

"You gotta stay strong," Freddy said. "That's the advice I give all kids your age. If you have the good luck to be healthy, then use that. Be able to punch their lights out before they can touch you."

She smashed the bag with a left hook.

"I'VE GOT A great idea," Nancy said as she met India and Benjamin at her door.

"Of course you do," India said. "Hi, Deborah. This is Benjamin Swan."

Deborah shook Benjamin's hand. "You're right, Nancy. He is cute."

India looked at Benjamin. He smiled.

They followed the two women through their large airy home, passing by shelves filled with pottery and ferns.

"You always see photos of artists painting naked women," Nancy said. "For my photo shoot, I'll be a naked artist painting a dressed woman."

Benjamin nodded. "Brilliant!"

"I like him," Deborah said.

Benjamin photographed Nancy nude painting a clothed Deborah. Nancy and Deborah flirted with Benjamin and walked comfortably from room to room, either naked or half-dressed. India admired their ease with their bodies. When it was Deborah's turn, she sat at a potter's wheel guiding a brown pot to completion. Nancy spread clay on Deborah's breasts, belly, and face, and Benjamin took pictures.

Afterward, the four of them had an early dinner. They discussed publicity strategies. Deborah had already set up interviews with the Vancouver, Portland, and Seattle papers and websites as well as several radio stations. She was going to put up a website where people could order the calendars, too.

"We're going to do a blitz a few days before Christmas," Deborah said. "They kept telling me it was impossible, so I pushed harder and it's going to happen. I predict we sell out before the new year."

BENJAMIN SPENT MOST of the evening at his computer, looking over his photographs. India fell to sleep finishing the biographical page; she didn't write a word about any of their sex lives.

Benjamin whispered her awake. "India, India Lake."

"Hello," she said softly.

He leaned over, picked her up, and carried her into the bedroom. Half-asleep, she took off her clothes. He kissed her face. She sighed. She still wanted him so much. Even half-asleep. Even when they were tired and hungry, she craved him. When she opened to him now, she felt as though she were in a dream and he was a part of it. She moaned sleepily, as he moved inside of her. In the dark she was not quite sure where he began and she ended. She knew that should terrify her, but it didn't. Not tonight. She thought of the poor Swan Maiden forced to marry the hunter because he had stolen her cloak. After watching Benjamin for the past two days, she was sure that if he knew where her cloak was, he would give it to her gladly and lay it across her shoulders, cheering on her transformation.

THE FOLLOWING MORNING, Rhonda waited for Benjamin and India in her own living room. Isaac was down in his workroom, Rhonda told them. She wanted to be photographed crocheting. She sat on the couch in her bathrobe. India and Benjamin arranged the pillows and blankets she had made around her. She told Benjamin to look away while she squirmed out of her robe. Then she put her crochet bag in her lap and held her latest work in front of her as she peered over her bifocals. India readjusted the pillows and blankets. Benjamin turned around and took the pictures.

"There is really something quite decadent about this," Rhonda said. "India, I have a box of chocolates over on the table. Can you bring it here?"

India got the open box and put it within Rhonda's grasp. Benjamin continued taking pictures as she reached for a chocolate or two.

When they were finished, Rhonda slipped back into her robe, pushed away the blankets and pillows, and stood. "I might just do that again."

MARLO SAT WITH her four Irish setters. It took a while to get the five of them to settle down. India felt as though she was with an entire troop of preschoolers. Finally, Marlo sat on the couch and the dogs jumped up with her and all five looked solemnly at the camera. Benjamin took his pictures.

PANSY, VIOLET'S MOTHER, was painting, her body the paint brush.

"Is that safe?" India asked as the woman poured violet-colored paint over her head.

"Sure," Pansy said. "All of my paints are food based. This one is almost all blueberry."

She walked to the canvas on the wall and rolled herself against it while Benjamin took pictures. Then she put the canvas on the floor, stepped into a vat of bright yellow paint, and made footprints on her body prints.

"Turmeric, onion, and some other non-toxic stuff," Pansy said.

Violet came in and watched for a few minutes.

"Thanks for helping out," India said to Violet. "How is the lunar part of the calendar coming along?"

"Good," Violet said. "I've done all the actual astrological stuff for the thirteen months. We'll show the phase of the moon each day, but the moon will be transparent. You know, instead of showing the New Moon as all black, it'll be gray so people can still write things in the spaces and be able to read them. We made the moons bigger than what you'd normally see in a lunar calendar. More like the size of the squares on a regular calendar—

only circles. Does that make sense?"

"Sounds very sensible," India said. "I e-mailed the biographical information to Clementine this morning."

Violet nodded. "Yeah, I got it. I wish I could pose. It looks like fun."

"Wait another twenty years, and you'll be ready."

"Have you done it yet?" Violet asked.

"I'm next," India said. "We're meeting tomorrow at five to choose the pictures. You coming?"

Violet nodded. "How's Jack doing?" she asked.

Benjamin had stopped taking pictures. Pansy dabbed paint onto the canvas with a paper towel.

"I haven't seen him lately," India said.

"He told me he didn't want to go out any more because you two were getting back together," Violet said.

"Really? When was this?" India asked.

"Not too long ago."

India looked at Benjamin. Violet followed her gaze.

"Maybe he said he hoped you'd get back together."

Benjamin walked up to them. "Ready?" he asked India.

"Sure. Thanks Pansy!" she called. "We'll see you both tomorrow."

When Benjamin and India went out to the car, the sun was shining. The day was cool, still almost like October.

"Any ideas where you'd like your photographs taken?" Benjamin asked as they got into the car.

"In bed waiting for you," India said.

"We don't need pictures for that."

"How about the pond then, on the rise of the slope. I'll crouch down and look up at the swans. You can take a photo of me and the swans."

"That would be beautiful," he said. "But it is cold, and we'll have to move carefully and slowly so we don't frighten the swans. Plus there is goose shit all over there."

"That's true," India said. "I have this blanket." She reached into the back seat and grabbed a small dark green blanket. "I could wrap myself in it and go up the slope, drop it on the ground so I won't be crouching in goose shit. Then I'll peek up at the swans and you can snap your pictures."

"Sounds good," he said.

India drove them the short distance to her home. Then they walked to the pond. Pink gold light was beginning to spread across the meadow. India kept herself hidden from the swans behind a wall of blackberry bushes while she quickly undressed. She threw her clothes on the barbed wire fence. Once she was naked—except for her boots—Benjamin draped the blanket around her shoulders.

India crept down the slope, crossed the ditch, and went partway up the other side of the slope. She raised herself up just enough so she could see the swans through the marsh grass. About ten of them were clumped up together near the edge of the pond. India ducked down again, took a deep breath, and laid the blanket on the ground. She sat on it, now naked, and pulled off her boots and socks. She glanced at Benjamin. He gave the thumbs up sign.

So far so good. The swans did not appear to be alarmed. India was not as cold as she thought she would be. She crouched, her hands on the blanket. Then she raised herself until she was looking at the swans. The cool air felt good on her face. Her skin tightened all over her body. She was so close to the ground she smelled its wet earthiness—and the marsh scent of rich black dirt. Ahhh, the swans: preening, eating, floating on water. Utterly wild. And she was with them, a part of this Natural Universe. She wanted to leap up and dance with joy.

She wanted to stay like this forever.

"I'm one of you," she whispered. "I am wild, too. Only—"

Only what? Had she lost her swan cloak? How? If she had it, would she put it on now and fly away with them when it was time to return to their Arctic home?

She smiled at her fantasy.

One of the swans looked at her. India stared back for a moment, then ducked out of sight. She grabbed her boots and socks and put them on. She picked up the now goose-shit covered blanket and ran—naked—down the slope and over the ditch to Benjamin Swan. He opened his arms. She dropped the blanket and flung herself into Benjamin's embrace.

"You are a sight," Benjamin said. He kissed her ear. "You're freezing. Come on. Get dressed so we can get you home, Swan Maiden."

"I NEVER WOULD have guessed one could get so tired

taking pictures of naked women," Benjamin said when they got back to India's house.

"You take a shower," India said. "I'll make us something to eat."

He nodded. India went into the kitchen and scrambled a few eggs, made toast and hot water, and carried it all into the bedroom.

She took off her clothes and sat on the bed eating. Benjamin came out of the bathroom, smiled, and took off his towel and sat on the bed with her.

With their backs against the wall, they ate.

"Wait until you see the pictures," Benjamin said "They are really good. Everyone is showing up at 11:00 tomorrow, right? I hope the weather holds."

"Yes, I got them all to come at the same time tomorrow, which is a miracle in itself. When we have to change a regularly scheduled POOL meeting it practically takes an act of Congress to get an agreement on a new time. Everyone has been very accommodating, and they will all wear something white as you requested."

India took Benjamin's empty plate and set it on top of hers on the night table.

"Lay down," India said. "I'm going to pleasure you."

Benjamin laughed and slid down on the mattress.

"Turn around," she said.

"Benjamin lay on his stomach. India straddled his butt and started rubbing his back. He moaned.

"That feels nice," he said.

India massaged his shoulders and back, his buttocks and legs. Then she sat with his feet on her thigh and rubbed his soles. She liked his body. Liked the feel of his skin against hers. He was beginning to become familiar to her. Their lovemaking was slower. She noticed him more instead of being completely lost in her pleasure. Although getting lost in ecstasy was the point, wasn't it? Or was it about getting lost in ecstasy with someone else? It couldn't be only those seconds of orgasm that mattered, could it?

She heard a slight snore coming from Benjamin.

She had never let anyone stay long enough to find out whether he snored or not.

Except Raymond and she could not remember if he had snored.

Benjamin shifted and turned onto his side. He smiled sheepishly.

"I was resting my eyes," he said.

"Uh-huh," India reached over to the chair, got her T-shirt, and slipped it on. "Come on, old man. Let's get some sleep."

THIRTEEN WOMEN WEARING winter jackets over long flowing white dresses, skirts, or slacks walked down the grassy meadow path. India walked amidst them, Benjamin behind them. The sun was out. The morning clouds in the gorge were slowly burning off, revealing snow touched mountain tops. The swans were gone—temporarily. India had seen them fly toward Franz Lake earlier in the morning.

When the women reached the outside of the holding pen, Benjamin said, "Do whatever you want in this area." He motioned to the pond. Try to stay fairly close together."

The women took off their coats and hung them over the fence. A few wore white hats. Together they walked toward the water. India smiled as she looked at them. They were so relaxed, ethereal and solid, breathy and earthy. Nancy came up to India and put her arm across her shoulders. India looked at her. She was dressed in a white cowboy hat, white shirt, white jeans, with white boots.

"Wow," India said. "You are quite a sight."

"She's my cowgirl," Deborah said, walking by.

Benjamin called to them. "Look this way."

"OK, girls," Rhonda called. "This is your shot at fame. Show him your pearly whites."

"Benjamin, we can't relax with all these clothes on," Clementine said.

"It's cold!" Nancy said.

"Let's be positive, ladies," Marian said.

"I'm positive it is cold," Nancy said.

Benjamin snapped the pictures. Then he went into the holding corral and momentarily disappeared from view.

"What's he doing?" Gina asked.

India shrugged.

Benjamin stood and came out of the corral carrying an armful of red roses. He walked over to the line of women.

He took out one rose and held it up to Beth.

"Thank you for showing me the secret life of moonlight."

Beth's hand shook slightly as she took the flower.

As he handed a rose to Rhonda, he said, "Thank you for teaching me what crocheting is all about."

"What is it all about?" Nancy asked.

"Chocolate," Rhonda and Benjamin said at once.

"Thank you for showing me your strength," he said to Freddy.

"—for your flowers," to Gina.

"—the true purpose of blueberries," to Pansy.

"—how Lady Godiva really looked," to Marian.

"—how to bake bread the right way," to Anna.

"—the magic of making soup sans clothes," to Clementine.

"Thank you for demonstrating how to be at ease in the world," he said as he handed one rose to Nancy and another to Deborah.

"—how fish really like to swim," to Cheryl.

"—that dogs are women's best friends," to Marlo.

"Irish setters certainly are," Marlo said.

Benjamin gave the last rose to India.

"Thank you," he said.

The women cheered and whistled.

"Thank you, Benjamin, for all of your care," Rhonda said. "You and India made us all feel comfortable. We count you as an honorary member of POOL."

"Here, here," Beth said.

"Now, let's wrap this up!" Nancy called.

"All right," Benjamin said. "Let me get a shot or two with you and the roses."

"Oh, so there was an ulterior motive for the roses,"

Nancy said. "It was all for the shot."

"Yep, it was all for the shot," Benjamin said. "So let's get a good one."

A CAR DROVE up to the meadow as the women left the pond. A familiar looking man got out and stretched. India put her arm across Rhonda's shoulder and walked her to her car. She waved goodbye as Rhonda drove past, then glanced back toward the pond, looking for Benjamin. He was talking to the man. India stopped and squinted. Who was he?

"We'll see you in a few hours," Nancy called as she and Deborah drove away.

India nodded. She went inside. She would have to remember to ask Benjamin later who that man was.

CHAPTER FOURTEEN

BENJAMIN SPENT THE rest of the Saturday in the garage apartment working on the photographs on his computer.

Deborah and Nancy came over late in the afternoon to finalize publicity plans. Gina and Anna arrived soon after.

"So far the calls we've been getting are very positive," Deborah said. "We're going to be busy giving interviews for a while. We'll have to decide who will do all that."

"Can't we just do the interviews with us all together?" India asked.

"That wouldn't be practical for very long," Gina said. "Most of us have jobs."

"Maybe a handful of us can do most of the interviews with the option that any of us can also participate," Nancy suggested.

Anna said, "Shall we tell them the news?"

Gina nodded.

"We contacted one hundred and seventy bookstores," Anna said. "Most of them in Portland."

"This took three days of ten hours a day each," Gina said. "Luckily I was able to take the days off, and Anna had the girls running the bakery. Our only break was getting naked for Benjamin!"

"We practiced our spiel on each other," Anna said, "then divided the list and went to town, so to speak. At first people were lukewarm, but when we mentioned we were going to be interviewed by the Oregonian or the Seattle Times, they got more interested. Remember, we have to give discounts to these bookstores. They usually get a forty percent discount. We gave them twenty percent."

"So how many orders?" India asked.

"Eight hundred and fifty calendars," Anna said.

"The feminist bookstore ordered ten copies," Gina said, "and offered to do a signing. If we do that, they'll order more."

"I couldn't get them to order a single copy of *Nature Girl*," India said, "but they'll buy a nudey calendar!"

"Don't be bitter," Nancy said.

"That only leaves one hundred and fifty for family and friends," India said. "Should we print more than a thousand?"

"Maybe," Deborah said.

"I'm paying for the printing," India said, "and I'm not

sure I can come up with much more money."

"You don't have to pick up the tab," Deborah said. "We'll get direct orders from the POOLers tonight. We should give ourselves a discount. How about if we can purchase the calendar for thirteen dollars each. If each POOLer got just ten copies, that's what?" Deborah wrote the figures on the paper in front of her. "That's almost $1,700 right there."

"Shouldn't each model get some free copies?" India asked.

"This is a fund-raiser," Nancy said. "We'll give two each. That sound good? The rest we have to buy. I certainly don't mind."

"This is very impressive," India said.

"And you thought POOL would never amount to anything," Nancy said.

"Not true," India said. "I thought we were a little disorganized."

"Now we're a finely honed organism," Nancy said.

They laughed.

Benjamin came in, carrying his laptop.

"Do we get a preview before everyone else arrives?" Anna asked.

"Absolutely," Benjamin said.

They cleared the papers off of the table and countertop. Benjamin opened his computer.

"I chose two pictures for each model," he said. "I thought that would save some time. When we're finished with the calendar, I'll make packets for each woman with prints of every shot I took."

He showed them India's photos first. She crouched on the banks of some unknown shore, feral-looking, taking a peek at the wild graceful swans. She seemed to ache with longing.

The women gasped.

Then Rhonda sat surrounded by blankets and pillows. The textures and patterns of the now black and white crocheted blankets were like artful soft sculptures. Rhonda reached for chocolate, with one eyebrow raised, as she looked over her glasses at the viewer. India could tell she was naked but not even a curve of her breast showed.

The women laughed.

Benjamin showed them picture after picture. Marlo and her dogs looked aristocratic. Benjamin caught Freddy as she punched the bag—captured the steely strength in her arm as it struck the bag, her other arm held back, shielding her breasts from view. Nancy painting Deborah while Deborah was dressed and Nancy was not was startling and funny. Deborah looked like an Earth goddess covered in clay with a pot between her legs.

Pansy's pictures were close-ups of her stomping joyfully all over her canvas. Cheryl was an Olympic goddess—a mermaid goddess diving into and leaping out of the water. Each of the photographs were mini-documentaries of the lives of the women. The last photographs he showed them were of Beth standing in the moon light. India's eyes teared. It was a portrait of a pure connection between Beth and Nature—with the Divine. Her arms were opened wide, as if receiving benediction from the moon.

"Wow," Nancy said. "You are an artist."

"A photographer is only as good as his subject," he said. "It was a pleasure." He looked at India. She nodded. He sighed and smiled.

"Let's put these in monthly order before everyone comes," Nancy said.

"India should be first," Deborah said. "Her photograph is all about the beginning of the connection to the wild, don't you think? And Beth's should be the last moon, the thirteenth moon."

"Absolutely," Nancy agreed. The other women nodded.

They spent the next hour choosing which of the photos would go in and in which order. They finished when Clementine and Violet arrived with the mock-ups of the actual lunar calendar. The two new women oohed and aahed over the photographs.

"Look at all of this astrological data," Deborah said. "You two did a fantastic job. It's in Pacific Standard Time. Viva the left coast!"

"What about the covers?" Clementine asked.

"Sorry," Benjamin said. "I forgot to show you. My brain is a little fried." He pulled up two more photographs. One was of the thirteen women standing by the pond, each holding what now looked like a black rose. Some of them looked at the camera, some at each other, a few of them held hands. Benjamin had taken a second photograph from behind the women as they walked toward the pond.

"I figure the first will be the front cover," Benjamin

said. "The one with you walking away could be the back."

"We are beautiful," Clementine said. "We look like Swan Maidens."

"Look," Violet said. "There are feathers around your feet, floating in the air, falling to the ground as though they're coming off of each of you."

"That's very clever of you, Benjamin," Clementine said. "It makes us seem like we are Swan Maidens."

Benjamin leaned forward and squinted at the screen. Then he shook his head.

"I didn't notice that before," he said. "But I didn't do it."

India looked at the photograph.

"You didn't touch it up or anything?" India asked.

He shook his head again. "I have no idea where those feathers came from."

"I guess this means we really are the Swan Maidens," Nancy said.

"Was there ever any doubt?" Deborah asked.

AFTER THE REST of the women arrived, Nancy and Deborah outlined the publicity plans and grouped the women into publicity teams. They handed out press releases and answers to questions about their goal in creating the calendar.

"It's better to say we're raising money to investigate possible wrong-doing by the county regarding their pesticide spraying procedures than to say we're raising money to sue their asses off," Deborah said. "If you're not sure how to answer a question, turn it over to someone else. You're most likely to be asked what it was like to get naked, stuff like that. Say whatever you like, but if you can steer it back to the purpose of POOL, then all the better."

"It's all in our brochure," Nancy said. She held one up and began reading, "We are dedicated to creating a healthy environment and protecting the ecology of our community. We want to do this by eliminating the use of pesticides and finding healthy alternatives to pest control situations."

"Daniel Salmonson warned me that this publicity could cause the pesticide companies to come after us," India said. "Try to be careful not to target any specific pesticide yet. We'll let Daniel do all that in court. You can talk about how pesticides get into our environment even in simple ways. Walking across a lawn where someone just put fertilizer, then walking into the library, say, and leaving residue on the carpet. Someone else comes in and carries that residue home to their house. They use pesticides in most schools. Here in the Shahalla schools they regularly have a pesticide applicator who comes in and sprays the classrooms as a preventative measure even if there is no indication of bugs. All that does is expose our children to greater risks for asthma, immune problems, and cancer."

"Can't we just say we did it because we wanted to get naked?" Gina asked.

Everyone laughed.

"Absolutely," India said. "Feel free to be yourselves.

That's what this is all about. It's a revolution, ladies. We want to be seen and heard!"

"Locally, the *Shahalla News* will have a story on us in Wednesday's paper," Nancy said. "We'll have a reception at the Recreation Center Thursday night and lunch with the seniors on Friday. After that, we figured you'd all want some holiday."

"We'll spend tomorrow putting it all together and doing a final edit, checking for stupid mistakes, etc.," India said. "We could use a couple extra pairs of eyes and hands. Then first thing Monday morning we're taking it to the printer. We'll pick it up and distribute it around Portland Tuesday morning. We'll need cars and volunteers to take the calendars around town."

"For those of you doing publicity," Deborah said, "we'll have press kits all ready to go, so we can put the calendars inside and take them with us. And we wanted to get everyone's calendar orders tonight so we can have some cash on hand for the printer. Anna and Gina have already sold eight hundred and fifty to bookstores."

The women cheered.

"OK," Nancy said. "Come give us your dough."

By the end of the evening, the POOLers had bought over three hundred calendars. India held up nearly four thousand dollars in cash and checks.

The women jumped up, cheering and laughing.

"I think we should do a print run of two thousand," India said. "If we sell them all, that's over $25,000."

"Go for it!" Rhonda said.

"All in favor?" India asked.

"Aye!" the group called out.

"Any nays?" India looked around the room and grinned. "The ayes have it!"

THE NEXT MORNING, India, Beth, Violet, and Anna worked on putting the calendar together. Meanwhile, Nancy, Deborah, Rhonda and Gina coordinated the publicity tour and distribution routes. At the end of the day, India looked up, and it was dark. Benjamin caught her eye, and she smiled. He seemed distracted, far away.

After the women left, India went into the bedroom to rest for a few minutes and didn't wake up until morning.

Benjamin and India ate oatmeal for breakfast, then bundled up and went into the morning. Dusk still had its fingers laced with dawn. They walked through the misty gray day until they saw the swans. This morning they looked ghost-like in the preternatural stillness, moving in the lake without the sound of any apparent locomotion. Benjamin put his arm across India's shoulder, and she leaned against him.

"If I haven't told you enough, let me say again how grateful I am for what you've done," India said, "and how impressed I am with your work. You didn't have to do any of it, and you did it all, and did it well."

Benjamin kissed the top of her head. "Thank you for asking. It has freed me up. I feel less. . . haunted, or something. I just feel better. Being around all of you women did it. And being able to take my pictures and make them into art is liberating."

"Now if we can get through the next few days," India said, "we'll be all right."

INDIA WATCHED BENJAMIN watch the swans. Something was already different. She could not quite pinpoint what. Almost as if they had woken up from a long sleep and saw each other for the first time: saw that they were strangers.

Benjamin and India went to Ecology Printing in Portland where they looked over the emailed mock-up with Polly. India thanked her for her help and said they would be back first thing the next morning.

Once they got home again, Benjamin went out to watch the swans. India took a long walk in the meadow.

She knew her life would not be her own for the next several days. She stood beneath the Seven Sisters and looked around. This was her life. She had chosen to do this calendar. She was trying to help protect the wild out here, the Earth beneath her feet. She put her arms around the closest tree sister and closed her eyes.

"This I love," she whispered. "This I love."

IN THE MORNING, India and Benjamin returned to Portland. The rest of the "convoy" was scheduled to meet them in the parking lot of a nearby mall.

Nervously, India got out of the car and walked into the print shop. Benjamin put a hand on her waist.

Polly looked up from across the room, smiled, and walked toward them. She pointed to the ground near India. India looked to her left. Four large boxes were piled near the door. On top was a calendar. "Natural Women." India picked it up. There they were on the cover. Like thirteen Swan Maidens disguised as women in white. Had they now all found their swan cloaks? Or had any of them really lost theirs? Cheryl had. She found it again when she dove into her husband's gift. Marian had lost hers for a while when she was sick but found it again out in the country with her animals and daughter. Clementine said she was adrift in the world until she started making soups with weird sounding names.

India picked up the calendar and opened it. There she was. Miss December 25 through January 23. She flipped the pages: Rhonda, Marian, Gina, Freddy, Pansy, Cheryl, Anna, Deborah, Clementine, Marlo, Nancy, and Beth as December 14 through January 12 of the following year.

"This is really something to be proud of, India," Polly said. "Don't be alarmed if you count an extra hundred or so. It's our donation to POOL."

"Thanks, Polly," India said. She took out her checkbook and paid for the balance of the order.

Benjamin and India carried the boxes out to the car. When they were finished, they got into the car and looked at each other—and started laughing.

"I can't believe we did it," India said. "It's beautiful!"

"It is," Benjamin said. He kissed her. "Thanks for inviting me along on the ride."

NANCY WAS LIKE a traffic cop at a six way stop. She had the calendars distributed to the other drivers within twenty minutes. She gave India her itinerary for the next couple of hours and put her in a car with Deborah, Marian, and Rhonda.

"You all are going to the Oregonian and KBOO," Nancy said. "We're scheduled at *Willie Week* and the *Columbian.* See you later."

India waved to Benjamin. He was going to be one of the drivers. He said he had had plenty of media coverage a year ago and was not willing to repeat that experience. He smiled and waved to India. Deborah drove off. Rhonda and Marian sat in the backseat looking at the calendar. India gazed out the window and wondered what she had gotten herself into. Suddenly she remembered why the strange man in the meadow talking to Benjamin had looked familiar. He was the same man who had sat in the back of the room at the meeting about the Dutch property. The man in the expensive suit. What had he wanted with Benjamin?

"Here we go, kids!" Deborah said. "Ready for the shame of fame?"

CHAPTER FIFTEEN

INDIA SPENT THE next two days going from interview to interview. Some she did in person, some on the phone. Apparently the media was tickled to do an "old ladies get naked" story before the holidays. Some of the reporters treated the women respectfully; others did not. India didn't care. She got to talk about the environment and how harmful pesticides were to more than just the pests.

"The bottom line is," one interviewer said, "you did what women have been doing forever: You took off your clothes for money."

India wanted to say, "And you've been doing what assholes have been doing forever: trying to intimidate women."

Rhonda opened her mouth first, however, and said,

"Well, honey, if you got it, I say sell it. You haven't felt anything until you feel polyester blankets all over your naked body while eating chocolate. Let me ask you this, young man, to what lengths would you go, if you were concerned that certain practices of your county might be responsible for poisoning our water and air? What would you do to find out why the frogs aren't singing?"

"That's because they croak, Rhonda," Marian said. "Not sing."

"That's what I'm saying," Rhonda said. "The frogs have croaked."

The interviewer tried to hide a smile.

"Is this calendar a way of flaunting your sexuality even though you are older women?" he continued.

"We wanted people to listen to us," India said. "We've been fighting this battle for years. We've been saying there is a problem with the environment. Nobody has been listening. We had to get their attention with something. This is what we came up with."

"As far as our sexuality," Marian said, "whatever that means, just because you're over thirty doesn't mean you stop having desires and feelings."

"For instance, I really have a desire for chocolate right now," Rhonda said.

The KBOO reporter asked them if creating the calendar was "an existential spiritual neo-realistic experience."

"Only to the extent that we became the purveyors of the ego-reality of the psycho-sexual pseudo-artistic venues," Marian answered.

"Excellent," the reporter said, nodding.

The POOL women looked at Marian. As the reporter asked another question, Marian leaned over to India and said, "It was part of a joke I heard."

"What our goal is," India said, again and again, "is to bring attention to our responsibility to our environment. Are we a part of our ecology or are we the destroyers of it?"

"An additional goal is to establish the fact that old broads rule," Rhonda said during one interview.

"That, too," India agreed, rolling her eyes. "And the more we rule the less we're going to put up with being disrespected or having the biosphere of this planet destroyed."

"In defense of Mother Earth," Marian said.

"Isn't that the battle cry of the radical environmental group Earth Firsters?" the interviewer asked.

"They stole it from us," Rhonda said. "We've been pissed off old ladies before most of them were even born."

"Speaking of theft," the interviewer continued, "haven't you stolen this idea from the English ladies?"

"They inspired us," India said. "So did the Salt Island women. We expanded on their idea and created our own *lunar* calendar."

"And why lunar?"

"Because we're lunatics," Rhonda said, "obviously. And because women are ruled by the moon, as it were. Or so many of our ancestors believed."

"Thoreau wrote about nature," India said. "Does that

mean you accuse anyone who writes about nature of thievery? There are dozens of nature calendars put out a year. Are they all stealing from each other? The English and Canadian women got naked for charity. So did we. We thank them for their courage and ingenuity."

Wednesday night, India stumbled home to a darkened house. Benjamin must be at the garage apartment, she thought. She was too tired to look for him. She checked her messages. One of them was from her boss at headquarters in Vancouver. She had not thought of work since she went on vacation. How odd. That place where she had spent most of her waking hours for ten years and she had left it without a backward glance.

Now she called her boss in Vancouver.

"Hey, Martha, what's up?" India said when she reached her.

"I saw the calendar," she said.

"Yeah, isn't it great?" India said. She sat on the couch and rubbed her face.

"We've seen several articles in the papers, including the *Shahalla News.*"

"I haven't read that one yet," India said. "The other articles seemed pretty fair. *The Oregonian* did a short press release, but they're doing a feature in A&E on Friday."

"India, I wish you'd told me you were doing this."

"It all happened really fast," India said. "Besides, I'm on vacation, and it's my private life."

"Still it would have been nice to be prepared. We've had quite a few phone calls."

India sighed. "You're right. I should have given you the heads up. I haven't been thinking about work."

"People are asking for your resignation," Martha said.

"What people?" she asked. "Did you tell them I have not done anything illegal, so I can't be fired?"

Martha was silent for a moment before she said, "Part of your responsibility as a branch librarian is to be an effective representative in the community. Do you think you can be effective after doing this calendar and then suing the county?"

"I guess we'll have to wait and see," India said. "If I can't do my job, I'll leave. I'm not going to stop fighting for those things that I believe in just because I have a job. Is there anything else? I'm tired and want to go to sleep."

"No, let me know how it all progresses, if you will," Martha said. "I bought several myself, by the way. They seem to be quite a hit. Have a good holiday, India."

"Goodbye," India said. She wished she had not sounded so defensive to Martha. She should have told her boss. Perhaps India was still resentful that they had made her go on vacation. So what if she had screamed at one patron in ten years? They should feel lucky she had not screamed at a lot more. Or taken her clothes off sooner. She smiled, then rubbed her face again. She was exhausted.

She picked up the papers on her kitchen table. There she was in the Northwest section of the *Columbian*: a photo of her and Rhonda holding up a calendar. She stared at herself. She looked so old and tired. Unattractive. She imagined Benjamin standing next to her. So young and gorgeous. She sighed. What an odd pairing they must seem. People probably snickered behind her back.

The phone rang. India picked it up.

"It's Daniel. Sorry to phone so late."

"Hey, what's up?" India asked.

"I had an interesting talk with Andrew Stephenson today," Daniel said. The county's attorney. "They have agreed to implement an IVPM policy for the county beginning this spring, and they'll hire a consultant immediately."

India felt a sudden burst of energy. "Daniel! That's fantastic! This is what we've been fighting for for years!"

Daniel was silent.

"What is it, Daniel? This is what we wanted."

"There's a catch," Daniel said. "They will implement the IVPM policy only if you and the POOLers do not object to the transfer of the Dutch property from the state to Aviary."

India laughed. "Well, that's simple. We weren't going to oppose it."

"Apparently they were worried you would, that you'd stir up public opinion against them."

"What? Why? They aren't doing anything to cause public alarm." She paused. "Or are they? Daniel. What's going on?"

"I'm not sure," he said. "But this has raised some red flags for me. I don't know Shahalla County laws that well, but I do know many counties have laws on

Kim Antieau

the books—some from a hundred years ago—that give broad powers to lumber companies."

"Wouldn't federal laws automatically supersede county laws?" India asked.

"In most cases," he said. "I won't have a chance to do a thorough check until after the new year—and it'll cost you. Nancy is good at ferreting out stuff from law books. Get her to go through the county's old laws. Just to be sure. Maybe nothing untoward is going on."

"OK. Thanks, Daniel."

India immediately called Nancy who agreed to do the research. By the time India hung up, she was feeling irritated and tired again. She thought about going to find Benjamin. Instead she turned off the lights and went to bed alone.

THE NEXT DAY, India sent out a pile of calendars to her family for holiday gifts. Then she and Benjamin went out to see the swans.

"Benjamin," India said as they walked to the path to the Seven Sisters, "I like the way you are with other people. You don't have that testosterone presence. You don't sit and wait to strut your stuff."

"Thank you, I think."

"I hope you know that you don't have to rescue me," India said. "You don't have to be the Swan Knight with me. You can just be you."

Benjamin nodded. "I think I figured that out. How about you? Do you feel like a Swan Maiden?"

"In the best possible sense," India said.

"Have you lost your cloak or found it?"

India shrugged. "I'm not sure what that means yet."

Geese flew noisily overhead.

"Daniel called last night," India said. "He told me the county will agree to our terms if we agree not to oppose the transfer of this property to Aviary Lumber."

Benjamin looked at her.

"I don't understand," he said. "Why would they ask for that?"

"I don't know," she said. "But we're going to find out. Sounds suspicious, doesn't it?"

He looked off across the pond. "It does sound strange."

They were silent for several minutes, then Benjamin said, "I'm going to leave in a few days to visit my folks for the holidays. You want to come with me?"

"Oh, I can't," she said. "There's too much going on here now."

"Nothing will happen over the holidays," he said. "Most of the POOLers are doing something with their families."

"I know. Still. I've been missing spending time with the swans while I've been doing all the POOL stuff. I think I want to stay here."

"Maybe next year?" he asked.

"When are you leaving?" India asked, not answering his question.

"Saturday. I'll try to be back for the new year."

"New Year's Eve has never been a big deal to me," India said. "Don't rush back for that."

"This New Year is a big deal," Benjamin said. "It'll be a new year with you."

"I don't want your family to think I'm stealing you away from them," India said.

"Are you kidding?" Benjamin said. "My mother will be so happy I'm seeing someone she'll weep."

"She doesn't want grand kids or anything, does she?" India said. "Because I ain't producing any."

"I guess this means you love me," Benjamin said.

"Why? Because I refuse to birth your children?"

He laughed. "No, because you're thinking about me in the long term."

India put her arm around his waist. "Where do your parents live?"

"They have a place on the coast, Newport, so we're all meeting there this year. Maybe you'll work on our swan book while I'm gone."

"You are such a nag," India said. "I'm working on getting through tomorrow at the rec center. Let's see if anyone throws rotten tomatoes at us."

"I want to take you someplace. It may be our last day without rain for a while."

"Where did you want to take me?" she asked.

"It's a surprise."

They walked to Benjamin's truck and got into it. He drove across SR14 and went up Duncan Creek Road. The truck bounced and weaved up past the creek until Benjamin stopped after the pavement ended. They stepped out into semi-darkness created by the forest. India heard running water. Dark green surrounded them. They walked a ways up the gravel road. After a few minutes, Benjamin pointed to a path and they walked up into the forest. Water dripped all around them. Here and there, the sunshine dripped through, too. Up the path. Over and around the broken red insides of rotting logs. Over vines, around living trees, across nurse logs.

"Where are we going?" India asked.

"Bigfoot's house," Benjamin said.

"Bigfoot doesn't have a house," India said.

"OK, Bigfoot's home," he said as they continued up the incline.

India stopped and stood in a shaft of golden sunlight for a moment. Then Benjamin pointed ahead of them. India followed his finger until she was looking at the largest patch of chickweed she had ever seen. She dropped down onto the light green plants. Drops of water clung to the tiny leaves. India took off her gloves and ran her fingers over the tops of the plant that spread out for several yards in all directions.

India laughed. "May I, may I?" she asked as her fingers stroked the leaves. Gently she picked off several leaves and popped them into her mouth. "Oh, Benjamin. They are so sweet. Did you know that at night the older bigger leaves fold up over the younger smaller leaves, protecting them from the cold? Birds love chickweed, too. How did you find this?"

Benjamin squatted next to her. "I looked for it. You said fairies dwelt where chickweed grows. After days of dealing with the media and the public, I thought you could use some non-human company. Bigfoot is essentially a North American fairy. I thought he might be hanging around here, too."

India continued to eat the chickweed. The forest was so quiet, except for that almost constant sound of water dripping and flowing from somewhere. India breathed deeply.

She reached for Benjamin's hand and kissed his fingers.

"Thank you," she whispered. She looked up at him. How could she have ever thought he was a stranger to her?

He smiled. His head blocked out the sun, and he was ringed in watery light.

India laughed. He looked so beautiful.

"Maybe you're Bigfoot," she said.

"Maybe I am," he said, dropping down beside her. She put chickweed in his mouth, then kissed his lips.

"Yes, I think you are. Bigfoot, the Swan Knight."

They returned to the pond where the sun was still shining. They watched from the west side of the pond. The swans ate wapato, cleaned themselves and each other, and floated on the water. Every once in a while one of the swans flapped her wings.

"So this is what swans do in winter," India said. "Eat, sleep, cuddle a bit, and hang out."

Benjamin laughed. "That pretty much sums it up, doesn't it? They breed when they're up in the arctic. In the summer they split up into family units and get rather territorial."

"They have sex and babies in the summer," India said,

"and congregate and eat in the winter?"

Benjamin nodded. "They seek out company in the winter."

India looked through her binoculars. "I wonder if they foment revolution in the winter like we do."

Benjamin laughed.

"That's what we could call our book," I said. "Swans in Winter."

Benjamin nodded. "Perfect."

When it got dark, they went indoors and ate soup and salad. They sat on the couch together and India asked Benjamin to show her how to use his camera. She had done some photography years earlier but had lost interest.

"The soul of photography is to bring to light that which you don't first see," Benjamin said. "The heart of photography is taking a picture of what you do see."

India took the camera from Benjamin. "That sounds easy," she said, laughing. "I suppose I do something similar with my stories. I try to expose what isn't seen but that which is known in our souls—or in our s-o-l-e-s as Rhonda would say."

"S-o-l-e-s?"

"She told me that if we're lucky we find a sole mate, someone with whom we can walk through life."

Benjamin nodded. "I agree with that."

"I dreamed once that you and I were walking together near the pond," India said. "I looked back and saw our footprints in the mud."

"We were sole mates?" Benjamin asked.

"I suppose we were," she said, "or mud mates."

They almost fell to sleep in each other's arms. Instead, they moved sleepily away from each other, with Benjamin's hand resting on India's hip.

THE NEXT DAY, India and the rest of the POOLers dressed up for their 7:00 reception at the Recreation Center. They recruited Isaac and Clem's husband Sammy to take the money; the women sat alongside the men, ready to sign calendars. Everyone except Nancy.

"Where is she?" India asked Deborah.

"She's coming," she said. "She was looking through the revised codes of Shahalla County."

At 7:15 only the spouses and a few family members wandered about the center eating cookies and sipping punch. Violet was trying to show Jack and Benjamin some belly dancing moves. Jillian, from the paper, snapped pictures.

About 7:30, people began streaming into the center and lining up to buy the calendars and have them signed. India waited for someone to yell at them and call them names. She had lived long enough in this community to know that something like that was not only possible but probable. People laughed and told jokes, danced a little to the music, and bought calendars. Some of the older men asked if they could go nude next year. Other women volunteered for next year.

India looked up from signing calendars several times to see people go up to Benjamin and shake his hand. She was glad he was getting some positive recognition for his photography. Maybe this experience would erase the memories of the last year when he was falsely accused.

After about an hour, the women were able to get up and mingle.

India saw Jack talking with Dick Lament. What on Earth was Lament doing there? India went over to them.

"Why are you here?" she asked Lament.

Jack looked down at his drink.

"Just seeing what's going on in my community," Lament said. "You know, India, you gals are hurting a lot of people with your allegations."

"We aren't gals," India said. "That's part of your problem, Dick. Get out of the middle ages. Do some research. Your pesticide policies are wrong and dangerous. Change them. If you don't, we'll take you to court. We aren't going away. Excuse me."

India wove her way through the crowd to Benjamin. He put his arm around her waist.

"What's wrong?" he asked.

"One of our commissioners is being an asshole," she said. "Nothing new."

Marian and Deborah joined them.

"Have you heard from Nancy?" India asked.

Deborah shook her head. "We did hear from some other people, though. The Chamber was a little upset with us, until they started getting inquiries about places to stay in the area. People are saying they heard those Natural Women live in Shahalla."

"Things happen so fast these days," India said.

"Rhonda's motioning to me," Benjamin said. "I'll be back."

As soon as he left, the other POOLers converged on the three women.

"What's going on?" India asked.

"We want to thank Benjamin," Anna said.

"He did an incredible job," Clementine said.

"Does he want or need anything?" Deborah asked.

"I don't really know." India watched him talking to Rhonda. "When he was a boy his mother used to tell him this story about the Swan Knight. His job was to find women who were not adjusting to the transition to patriarchal times and help them in any way he could. He said he identified with the Swan Knight. Remember that story of the Swan Maidens? They took off their swan cloaks and left them beside the pond while they danced in the wild. A hunter steals one of the cloaks and forces the Swan Maiden to marry him until she finds her cloak and flies away from him. Benjamin related to that story, too. He's the Swan Knight looking for the Swan Maiden's cloak, trying to help her find that lost part of herself."

The other women stared at her.

"What? You asked," India said.

"We thought maybe we could buy him a toaster oven," Marian said.

"That's a beautiful story, really," Clementine said.

"Yeah, he's our Swan Knight," Deborah said. "He helped us do what we needed to do. Let's get him one of those varsity jackets and have them write 'Swan Knight' on the back."

"Yes," Marian said. "A cloth one. White, with black trimming."

"It might look even more striking if it's black with white trimming, including the Swan Knight lettering," Deborah said.

"That sounds good," Gina said.

"Happy Solstice," Pansy said.

"Yes," India said. "Happy Solstice."

"I heard it is really snowing in Idaho," Clementine said. "Record snowfall."

"We'll be all right," Marian said.

Benjamin returned to India's side. "Plotting another revolution?" he asked.

"No," she answered. "Tidying up the loose ends of this one."

India spotted Nancy coming through the door. She excused herself and hurried toward her.

"Where've you been?" India asked.

"You won't believe it," Nancy said. "Daniel was right. There is an old code from 1886. It says that any land owned by a lumber company within ten miles of the Town of Shahalla is automatically part of the city."

India shook her head. "So what? They still can't do anything."

"You don't understand," Nancy said. "If the land is part of the city limits of any city or town in the Columbia River Gorge it is *exempt* from the Scenic Act. India, they can put up a mill. They can even put up a paper plant. They can do whatever the hell they want."

India felt like she couldn't stand. She backed into the

nearby wall for support.

"This can't be true." India said.

"I just got off the phone with Daniel," Nancy said. "I read him the statute, after I looked through all the other codes, to see if it had ever been rescinded. It never had been."

"And you think Aviary Lumber knew?" India asked. She shook her head and answered her own question. "Of course they knew."

India glanced over at the crowd. Several people were looking at them.

She took Nancy's hand and led her out of the rec room and back toward the office.

"This will ruin Turtle Pond, the swans, the meadow," I said. "The air! If they put up a paper plant, none of us will be able to breathe the air. How could I have been so stupid to believe this transfer was OK?"

"We wanted it to be all right," Nancy said. "We've got our hands full trying to stop them from continually poisoning us with pesticides."

Jack came around the corner.

"You bastard," India said. She strode toward him and raised her hand to strike him. Nancy grabbed her.

"India!" she said.

"How could you do this to me?" India said. "To our community!"

"What are you talking about?" Jack said, his face white.

"We found out what Aviary Lumber really wants with the Dutch property," Nancy said.

India could hardly see she was so angry and stunned. She tried to catch her breath.

"I still don't know what you mean," he said. "India?"

"They're going to build a mill or a paper plant," Nancy said. "That's why the county wanted this deal to go through. The amount of taxes they can collect from a plant or mill will be a great deal more than what they'd get from just a piece of wilderness. Aviary probably greased some palms to get this deal. Did they grease yours, too, Jack?"

"I don't understand," Jack said. "They can't build a mill or plant. That would violate the Scenic Act."

"All land owned by lumber companies within ten miles of the city limits automatically becomes part of the city," Nancy said. "It's an old statute. Obviously Aviary and the commissioners knew about it."

"India, you can't believe *I* knew about this?" Jack said.

She stared at him.

"You told me you investigated this," she said.

"I did," he said. "I didn't go back and look at all the old laws! I had no reason to. I love that land, too."

India shook her head. "This is what you meant when you said there was more going on than I knew."

"No, that's not it."

"Then what!"

Jack shook his head. "No, I don't want to do it this way. I—I." He sighed and rubbed his face. "I think Benjamin may have known about this. He's . . . his family owns Aviary Lumber."

India's eyes widened. "What?" Now she felt like she was going to be sick.

"I just thought it was a weird coincidence that he got the grant the same time his family decided they wanted this piece of property. His brother was at that meeting. He was sitting in the back of the room. In the blue suit."

India remembered the man.

Benjamin came around the corner with Deborah.

"Are you guys all right?" Deborah asked.

"Benjamin," India whispered. "Is this true? Does your family own Aviary Lumber."

"Yes," he said. "But—"

"Did they ask you to come here and spy on us? Did they ask you to get friendly with me."

Benjamin stared at her for several moments. India wanted to cry or scream. *Please let him say, "No."*

He said, "Yes, they did—."

"So you lied to me!" she said. "From the very beginning. You let me get close to you. You let me believe in you! You sonofabitch."

"India," Nancy said. "There must be more to it."

India hurried past Benjamin and out the door. She tried to find her car, but she couldn't see it. Find it. Tears blurred her eyes. She reached into her pocket for her keys.

"India." Jack was at her elbow. "Come on. You can't drive."

"No," she said, jerking away from him. "I can. I can. Where's my car?"

"Let me." He gently led her to his car. She got inside and leaned against the passenger door. He started the car and drove away from the county building. India caught a glimpse of Benjamin coming outside.

"Take me to your house, Jack. I don't want to go home."

At Jack's house, India stumbled into the bedroom and fell onto the bed. She began to cry. She cried until she fell to sleep.

INDIA OPENED HER eyes as Jack kissed her forehead.

She sat up. He held out a cup of hot water for her.

"I feel terrible," she said, taking the cup.

Jack sat next to her.

"Like I have a hangover and the flu," she said. "I feel so stupid. I really believed he loved me."

"Maybe he did," Jack said.

"Why didn't you tell me that Benjamin was part of Aviary Lumber?" she asked.

"First, Aviary Lumber wasn't a part of anything when Benjamin first came," he said, "and then I didn't think it was important. Benjamin has never been part of the family business. And Benjamin asked me not to tell you. He wanted to tell you about his family himself."

"How could you do that to me?"

"I didn't know about the rest," he said. "I didn't know his family had asked him to spy on you or anyone else. I didn't know what Aviary wanted to do with the property. Nancy phoned while you were sleeping. They've called an emergency meeting for after Christmas. All the par-

Kim Antieau

ties will be there."

India nodded. She set the cup on the bedside table and rubbed her eyes. "You must think I am such a fool. This old lady with him, with Benjamin. Everyone must think I'm a fool." She closed her eyes. How could he have done that to her? It had all seemed so real. So true. True to the bone. She wanted to scream. "You have no idea how much this hurts."

Jack put his arm across her shoulder. "Yes, I think I do."

"I think I'm going to be sick," she said.

She ran to the bathroom and threw up. She rinsed her mouth out and splashed water on her face. She looked at herself in the mirror.

"What an idiot," she said.

She walked back into the bedroom. Jack looked up at her.

"You are beautiful," he said. "I've always thought so."

She smiled wanly.

"Can we just lay together, Jack? Would that be all right?"

"Sure," he said. He stretched out across the bed, and she lay next to him, resting her head on his shoulder. Her stomach still lurched. Jack felt all wrong. His smell. His shape. She thought she would be sick again.

No, she told herself. This is Jack. Jack. He loved her. He knew her, and he loved her. It was all right. All right.

She closed her eyes and began to cry.

She awoke in the middle of the night. Jack lay next to her, asleep, still clothed. She smiled grimly and got up.

She couldn't stay here. It wasn't fair to Jack.

She went into the living room, wrote Jack a note, put on her coat and went into the cold night. Her house was only a mile or so away. She could do it.

She stepped onto the dark highway. No one around. She walked, shuffling her feet as if she were drunk or not quite herself. She heard a bird and looked up. The sky was bright with stars. A shadow flew overhead. She walked to Beacon Rock. She stood at the bottom of the steps remembering Benjamin telling her he had walked to the top in the middle of the night. She wondered if she could do it. Finally she shook her head and kept going. He had probably lied about that, too.

After a while, she saw car lights in the distance coming toward her, so she stepped off the pavement and went down the nearest driveway. She knew she could climb the fence here and get into the meadow. She could walk the rest of the way home on the Dutch property.

She hopped over the fence, fell, got up, and continued walking. The grass crunched beneath her feet, her weight breaking the green icicles. She walked by the woods that hid the chickweed and giant ant hill and to the center of the meadow. In the near distance, the Seven Sisters were gray reminders of another life. A coyote howled.

India screamed. She opened her mouth and howled her anger and hurt. She screamed until she was hoarse. Then she howled like a coyote, until the two of them were singing together. Until she started to laugh and cry

Kim Antieau

at the same time.

"Nature's child!" she cried out. "Born to be wild."

The cold air felt good in her lungs. Snow began to fall.

"Good night, Coyote," she said.

She walked until she heard the swans. They chuckled, chortled, and sang to one another. None of them moved or even seemed to notice as she walked by them. She hurried down the path, out to the road, and then to her house. Benjamin's truck was parked outside her garage.

How dare he still be here, she thought. She quietly unlocked her door and went inside. She bolted it shut and put on the chain. She glanced at her answering machine. Twenty calls.

She opened the machine, took out the cassette, and pulled on the tape until it was a sprawled mass of brown and black at her feet. Then she got a pair of scissors and snipped the tape into several pieces.

After she cleaned up the mess, she went to sleep.

CHAPTER SIXTEEN

THE NEXT MORNING, Christmas Eve, India opened the curtains to find a world draped in snow. The blackberry bushes were completely covered. Evergreen branches were weighed down by the snow. India got dressed and trudged through the foot of snow toward the pond. Benjamin's truck was gone. Mallards quacked at her intrusion and paddled away from her on the unfrozen pond. A great blue heron flew from a perch India had not noticed. At the east end of the pond, the swans ate. Relieved, India walked back to her house. Everything was storybook lovely. If she walked around that bend in the road, she was certain, she would find a gingerbread house. The light was almost milky, filtered through the clouds and bright snow. India stood in the silence in front of her house for a few minutes before going inside.

She spent the day napping. Jack called a couple of times. The clumpy snow fell slowly, silently. Every few hours, India heard the plows out on SR14.

After dark, India tramped through the snow to Rhonda's house for her annual Christmas Eve/Hanukkah/Yule/Kwanzaa party.

Isaac greeted India at the door with a kiss and pointed to the buffet table. The house was full of people, despite the snow. India walked through the crowd looking for Rhonda. She found her in the open kitchen slicing a loaf of bread.

"Anna brought this. I love her bread. How are you?"

"I'm great," India lied, looking around the noisy room. "It seems your party is a great success as usual."

"People are abuzz over the calendar," Rhonda said. "I had Nancy bring some to sell. This was a great inspiration you had. Who knew we could get organized and do something like this?"

"It's what I always wanted for us," India said.

"Isaac!" Rhonda put the plate of sliced bread on the sill between the kitchen and living room and pointed to it. She began slicing another loaf. "I know you have tried to get us up and going. I never really understood what you were after before. But we had confidence in you for this project. We knew you could pull it off."

India laughed. "I didn't do it. We all did."

"You were the catalyst," Rhonda said. "The idea person. And good for you! Nancy told me everything, you know. About Aviary and the statute. Daniel will fry 'em.

Don't worry. They won't get away with it. Though I can't believe Benjamin had anything to do with it. Here. I don't think Isaac heard me. Take the bread out."

India did as Rhonda asked. Then she wandered through the house stopping to talk with friends. Eventually she made a plate for herself and went downstairs and watched part of *A Christmas Story* with Isaac and Charlie. The three of them shared a bottle of wine.

When the movie was over, Isaac and Charlie went upstairs.

"Hello."

India looked up. Jack came down the stairs. She smiled. It was good to see him. She patted the seat next to her.

"How did you get here in the snow?"

He shrugged. "I'm a man. What can I say?"

She laughed. She leaned over and kissed him. He responded.

"I guess you're feeling better," Jack said.

India kissed him again. She liked the feel of him so close to her. She wanted him. Wanted to take him home.

"Have you spoken to Benjamin?" Jack asked.

India moved away from him. "No."

"I think you should," he said. "He stopped by before he left. He has some things to say."

India looked at Jack. "I thought you wanted me to get away from him. I thought you wanted us to be together."

"I do," he said gently, "but not because of a misunderstanding. I told you he's never been a part of the family business. You never gave him a chance to explain. You just assumed he was guilty. It was almost like you wanted him to be guilty."

"That's just stupid," India said. "Why would I want him to be guilty? Why would I want to be made to look like a total ass? Jack, are you going to come home and make love with me or not?"

"I want you to have all the facts," Jack said. "Then you can decide which of us you want."

"I want you," India said. "Right now I want you."

"As charming an invitation as that is," Jack said, "I can wait until you're sure."

"Goddamn it, I am sure," India said.

Jack laughed. "Have you been drinking? I never thought I'd see the day."

"It was *organic* wine," India said, grinning. "No pesticides. Viva la . . . wine."

Jack kissed her mouth. He moaned as he pulled away. "I better go, though I know I'm going to kick myself for this tomorrow."

"Come home with me and I'll kick you in the morning," she said.

Jack laughed and went back up the stairs.

India walked home alone. It was no longer snowing. The street lights made the snow gleam and sparkle. India walked to the meadow. She could not see the swans, but she heard their murmuring. She listened for a few minutes under the cold dark moon sky, then she went home. She lay alone in her bed for a long while, watching the ceiling spin, before she was able to fall to sleep.

Christmas morning it was snowing again. India called her family who were all gathered in Michigan this year. She listened to her teenaged niece complain about this week's boyfriend while she watched the snow fall outside. After she hung up the phone, she cried.

Midday the electricity went out. India went into her bedroom—the warmest room in the house—and lay on her bed. She knew she should close the curtains, but she liked watching the weather. The wind had picked up and white-out conditions were developing.

She gazed at her hands. They looked like the hands of a young girl. She still weighed the same as she had when she was thirteen years old and had reached her current height. Of course gravity had taken its toll over the years, and her breasts were not as high on her chest as they had once been, though she had never been able to lay claim to being perky. The skin sagged over her knees a bit, too. She saw the veins in her legs. She smiled. This ol' gray mare ain't what she used to be. She had hated what she had become for so long. She had given up on herself when she thought everyone else had. That had not been very honorable. That had been when she needed herself the most.

Now she was finding ecstasy in her body again. Not because of Benjamin. Maybe he had been the catalyst, like Rhonda said she was for the calendar. Maybe it was the belly dancing class. She rolled over. She was not sure what had happened. She only knew she felt wild again. Like herself as a child running through the woods feeling everything so intensely. Watching the mother and baby mice inside a rotten log. Leaning too close to a rattler in full dance. Riding bareback on her pony down the dirt back roads. Lying on a bed of moss and feeling its gentleness. The smell of ozone just before it rained. The sound of robins bringing dusk to the yard.

Ahhh, wilderness.

India had wanted to feel this way forever.

And then she learned the truth about Benjamin. How he had never really wanted her. How their entire relationship had been a lie.

But did she know the truth? Jack claimed she didn't. Said she wanted to find an excuse not to be with Benjamin. Such rubbish. She didn't need to make up an excuse. She loved him. She had thought they would be together forever. She sighed. And that was terrifying. To love someone so much that you weren't sure you could live without them. She breathed deeply. Yet here she was living without. Breathing.

The electricity came back on. Two feet of snow had fallen, at least.

The next morning, India turned on the television. SR14 and Highway 84 on the Oregon side were temporarily closed because of ice at the west end of the gorge near Vancouver and Portland. India curled up on the couch and read. She went up to the garage apartment once. Benjamin had left behind the swan pictures for their book Swans in Winter.

Daniel called. "Andrew Stephenson phoned me. He wanted to know if the POOLers were serious about the suit. He said he was calling me as a favor, to let us know that the commissioners were against you. I told him any publicity was good publicity—for our cause. I told him we would take them to court over Aviary Lumber, too. I could hear him turn pale. I think they're running scared, India. Plus a reporter for the *Columbian* called. They're sending out an investigative team to Shahalla County. They want to talk to the people who claim they saw water sources being sprayed. I called Jessica and Stuart Olson and the O'Neills to see if I could give out their names, and they agreed to be interviewed. The ball is moving, India, the ball is moving."

Later India called Jack.

"Sorry about the other night," India said. "I guess I was drunk."

"That's all right," he said. "I'm black and blue from kicking myself."

India smiled. "Your place OK?"

"Yeah. But I'm stuck here. I wish I hadn't gone home. I'd rather be stuck there with you."

"Yeah, that would have been nice."

"Call if you need anything," he said.

"See you later." She hung up. *I need you*, she wanted to scream. She looked out the window. She needed something.

Later the phone lines went down. The wind howled. Snow piled up. They reopened 84 and 14, then shut them down again.

The next day, the snow stopped, but the wind didn't. The phones came back up. Then midday it was suddenly very still. India went outside for a few minutes. The pond was frozen. The swans were gone. The air tasted different.

Soon after, the freezing rain began. India quickly called around the Landing to make certain Rhonda and Isaac and her other neighbors had enough wood and food. Freezing rain usually meant no phones or electricity. India heard the frozen rain pelting the house. She opened the door once. Everything was covered in thick ice. Nothing moved on the roads. The radio said they had stopped train service on both sides of the river. Highway 84 and SR14 were sheets of ice.

India tried to leave the house once to check on Rhonda and Isaac, but her feet found no traction on the glaze of ice over the snow.

As she fell to sleep that night, she heard the ice-covered branches of the now bent-over birch next to the house clink, clink, clink against the roof, like some kind of giant wind chime.

India awakened cold. She switched on the lamp but got no light. The electricity was out again. She had no independent heat source. Rhonda and Isaac had a wood stove, but it was too icy to walk that far. She could crawl, but she would probably freeze before she got to their house. She got up and retrieved several blankets from her closet and spread them over her bed. She put on a pair of pajamas and a sweater and got into bed. She remembered that girl scout camping trip when the scout leader yelled at her for telling stories and getting cold. She had not been able to sleep that night.

She closed her eyes. She would have to sleep this

night. She couldn't stay awake thinking about the Dutch property, Benjamin, Jack, or the mess of her life. She had to sleep. Nothing else to do.

In the morning, India had electricity again. The day was cold and windy. She felt housebound and lonely. The house shook. The windows rattled. The phones worked intermittently.

The next morning, India awakened to the sound of water dripping from her roof.

The temperature was rising.

She opened her front door. Water ran down the street. It was raining. The world was soggy white.

The temperature was rising too fast.

India got dressed and went outside. She could still hardly walk because of the ice which now had a stream of water running over it. When she got back into the house, the phone was ringing. She picked it up.

"Indy!" Rhonda cried. "The pipes burst, and Isaac fell. He's hurt. I called the ambulance, but they said it'll be a while. There have been two landslides on 14, and they're caught behind one."

"Is Isaac in the house or is he outside?"

"No, he's here. He got the water turned off. He fell coming up the steps. But he's inside."

"Is he lucid?"

"Yes! His pulse is good. He's pale though and his hip is hurt. He's eighty years old, India!"

"What did the ambulance people say?"

"They said to wait." Rhonda sounded terrified.

"I'll be right over," India said.

She hung up the phone, went to the closet and took out two brooms. She got a hammer and nails and pounded a nail into the handle end of each broom until the nail stuck out about an inch.

Then she went out into the icy rain. She punched the nailed handles into the ice to keep herself from slip-sliding away. Within minutes, she was drenched, but she did not fall. She watched her feet as she traveled the short distance to Rhonda's house—the short distance that took her nearly twenty minutes to traverse.

As soon as she was inside the house, she pulled off her coat, hat, mittens, scarf, and boots: All were soggy wet. She hurried over to Isaac. He sat in his chair drinking coffee. Rhonda stood over him.

"You OK?" India asked.

"My hip hurts," Isaac said, "but I'm not sure I need an ambulance."

"Someone needs to look at you," Rhonda said.

The phone rang. Rhonda hurried to it. "What?" she said. "What should we do then? I don't care about that. He needs to see a doctor! Yes, yes, we can try." She hung up. "The Shahalla ambulance is in a ditch. The other is at another call. They said we could drive Isaac to the landslide, though they were not recommending it. The Clark County ambulance is about ten miles from the slide. They can meet us there."

"I'll take you," India said. "We can take your car. It'll take too long to get mine. Isaac, do you think you can get to the car?"

He nodded.

"Give me the keys. Get your coats on."

Rhonda reached into her purse, got her keys, and threw them to India. India ran down the stairs and went into the attached garage. Once inside the car, she hit the garage opener. She started the car and eased it out onto the road. It slipped a bit on the ice but was steadier than India had been walking. She left the car running in front of the door, got out, and ran up the stairs which were now free from ice.

Rhonda held up an umbrella as she and Isaac walked out. Isaac grimaced. India gave him her arm, and he leaned heavily against her. Slowly they went down the steps. Rhonda opened the car door. Flinching, Isaac slid into the front seat. Rhonda got in the back. India hurried around the car, slipped once and pulled herself up again. She was so cold she could barely flex her fingers. She got into the driver's seat and drove away from the house.

The car fish-tailed some, but the road got better when India turned onto SR14. The rain came down in sheets. She drove in the ruts in the hard ice. Wilderness surrounded them on all sides, drenched, wet, slip-sliding wilderness. They were not safe in this car from the shifting world.

Inside the car was quiet. India heard Isaac's breathing, the slip-slap of the windshield wipers.

The miles went by slowly. The world seemed to be melting. Water poured off of the roadside hills, making streams through what was left of the snow and ice. The ditches spilled water, becoming mini-rivers. St. Cloud Creek was flooding over the road. India drove carefully around the water. A mile later, they came upon the land-slide: a conglomeration of toppled trees, brown mud, and rocks. On the other side, ambulance lights flashed.

India stopped the car, grabbed the umbrella, and got out. The wind blew the rain into her face. She should have put on her coat no matter how wet it had been. She ran to the landslide. Several men dressed in orange stood near the toppled hill. India skirted the debris and went to the other side where the ambulance waited. She knocked on the steamy window.

A woman rolled down the window.

"Are you here for Isaac Stein?" India asked.

The woman nodded.

"I've got him in the car."

The two EMTs got out of the ambulance, took a stretcher from the back, and followed India around the slide to the car.

India got into the car.

"How are you doing, Mr. Stein?" the male EMT said when he opened the door.

"I'm a little sore," Isaac said.

India tried to listen while they talked with Isaac, but her teeth were chattering. Rhonda threw her a blanket from the backseat.

"I'm going with them," Rhonda said. "You take the car. We'll stay in town. I don't know what the hell we're doing stuck out here in the boonies anyway. I'll call you."

Rhonda took the umbrella. The EMTs put Isaac on a stretcher. Rhonda held the umbrella over her prone husband as they carried him away. The wind turned the umbrella inside out. Rhonda struggled with it, then finally let it go. The wind took it across the road. India thought about getting it, but she was too cold.

India drove back to Rhonda's and got her coat. Then she drove to her house. She sat in a hot bath for an hour.

When she finally got out, she turned on the television. Nearly every river in southwestern Washington and northwestern Oregon was either near flood stage or was flooding. The Columbia River was expected to be at flood stage in eight hours as the snow melt in Idaho and Washington coursed into the river. Towns along the coast and Highway 26 in Oregon were already flooding.

Rhonda called. Isaac's hip was not broken, but it was badly bruised. They wanted to keep him overnight to watch for blood clots.

India phoned Jack and told him about Isaac.

"I've never seen so much water," India said. "It's everywhere."

"I called the police," he said. "SR14 is closed. They've had another slide on 84, too. They think it'll be days before either is open again."

"I feel strange," India said. "One thing after another seems to keep happening even though most of my time is spent waiting, listening to the weather. We're going through six months of changes in less than two weeks. This can't last too much longer, can it?"

India was not able to get to sleep until well into the night. In the morning, things felt different again. She looked out the window. The swans were still gone. She put on her coat, stepped outside, and looked toward the river.

"Oh my gawd," she said.

The Columbia River had risen over night, higher than India had ever seen it. It was well past the dock, and twenty feet up the boat ramp with the riparian trees completely flooded.

Brown. Everything was brown. Everywhere she looked she saw water. Another twenty feet and the river would come up to the road. And into her back yard. That could not happen. It had never happened. She looked at the Strand's house down the road from her. It was perched above the river. They had built it above the hundred year flood plain level.

And the river was lapping ten feet below their house.

Was this the hundredth year?

India ran to the meadow and looked toward the marsh where Benjamin's tent had been.

The meadow was now part of the river. The water covered the barbed wire fences at the lower end of the marsh.

"Damn." That meant injured wildlife.

She looked toward the pond. She was glad the swans were gone. She walked to the ditch where she and Benjamin often stood to watch the swans—the ditch she had traversed to crouch naked before the swans. It was now filled with water.

Rain pelted her face. India looked around. It seemed the world was now made of water.

CHAPTER SEVENTEEN

HOUR BY HOUR, the Columbia River rose. India saw the Strands standing on their back balcony watching the waves lap closer and closer to their bottom floor. The river crept up India's backyard.

Late in the day, the water crested the top of the marsh and covered the upper fences, too. Thirty feet of "dry" ground separated the pond from the river. Ducks and geese bobbed on the pond.

The rain continued. The swans flew back to the pond. India watched them all land on the water almost at the same moment.

The water rose.

At midnight, India went over to the Strands to help the Volunteer Fire Department sandbag. The river was inches from flooding the house. Dick Lament nodded to her as he hooked up flood lights. They turned on the pumps when the water began seeping through the bags.

For hours, India helped fill bags with dirt and place them on the sand wall. Nancy, Freddy, and Pansy joined the volunteers.

Toward dawn, Lament came up to India.

"Thank you for helping out," Lament said. He shook his head. "This is Nature, India. This is the wilderness you worship. It isn't pretty, is it? We need to do what we can to master this kind of situation. To tame her back."

"Yes, and we've succeeded so well at mastering Nature, haven't we?" India said. "Shit happens, Dick. We can't control everything."

She wanted to ask if he had ever heard of global warming. She wanted to explain to him that the kind of landslides they had in this area were due in part to unstable land caused by clear-cutting and overdevelopment.

She didn't. She sighed. She was not going to convince him of anything.

"I hope you and your family are safe through all of this," she said.

"Thanks, India, I appreciate that."

"By the way, we know about the statute, Dick," India said. "We know that Aviary was planning on building a mill or a plant of some kind on the Dutch property. How could you even consider destroying this land for money?"

"The county is nearly broke," Lament said. "We need to do something to bring in jobs, to bring in some money to help provide services. I'm not ashamed of trying to accomplish that."

"You should be ashamed for not telling us the whole truth," she said. "That's your job. Not to hide things from the public but to act in the best interests of the people."

"I believe I was doing exactly that," he said. "We wanted to get as much accomplished as possible before you environmentalist came in and got everyone all riled up."

"Jesus, Dick," India said. "Could you be a bigger asshole?"

India shook her head as he walked away, rain and water splashing up all around him. Nancy slapped India on the back.

"He is an asshole," she said. "Let's show them all. Let's do an un-rain un-flood dance."

"You lead the way," India said.

The women walked toward India's house. They stopped at the mid-way point and looked at the river.

"OK, Rain and Wind and Weather! It's enough!" Nancy shouted. "We give! This is causing too much destruction! You can please stop now."

"Who is she talking to?" Freddy asked.

Pansy shrugged.

"To the river and rain," Nancy said. "Now dance the un-rain dance."

The four women began dancing, splashing around to the beat of the un-rain dance.

Then they ran to India's house. She dried their clothes and fed them toast and hot chocolate.

"Have you spoken to Benjamin?" Nancy asked.

India shook her head. "I don't want to talk about it."

"OK." Nancy held up her hands. "But you should talk to him. At least once, before you call it quits."

"I have called it quits," India said. "That's the end of it."

"Too bad," Nancy said, shrugging. "He was a nice guy."

The women left before the sun came up.

Just about then, the rain and wind stopped. The Columbia River was a foot from India's house. She walked to the pond.

The river had eaten the pond. Swallowed it whole. The river was a giant brown lake stretching from here to everywhere.

India went back inside and watched the aftermath of the massive floods on TV. People piloted boats into their homes and businesses and talked about Mother Nature getting her due.

It was New Year's Eve and southwest Washington was declared a disaster area.

India watched the swans float on the giant lake.

"Beware," she whispered. "Beware. They will steal your cloak."

She watched Benjamin's loner swan—the one he said reminded him of her, with the gray neck and head—scrounge the north end of the pond for wapato. The water was too high, though; she came up empty. India wondered why the birds stayed.

The river crested.

The water level started going down.

The Department of Transportation cleared the avalanches on 84 and SR14. India was exhausted. Something about having life be so elemental for so many days had tired her out. It exhausted everyone she spoke with.

Nancy and Deborah brought Rhonda and Isaac home from the hospital. Both were too tired to do anything. India took care of dinner. They ate it silently, sitting in their living room.

Isaac said, "I've never seen it like this before."

"Have you called all the POOLers?" Rhonda asked when India got up to leave. "To see if they're all right."

"No. Should I?"

"Maybe."

"I will. I'll do it when I get home," she said.

She kissed them goodbye and hurried home. She didn't know why she had not thought of calling the POOLers herself. She had isolated herself in this island of her home for days.

She called everyone she had not spoken to since the weather had started. They were all safe, dry, and warm.

"I'm sorry I didn't phone earlier," India told Beth.

"I heard you've been flooded down there," Beth said. "I've been fine. We'll get together as soon as this all settles down."

India hung up the phone after their goodbyes. Then she stood looking out her window into blackness and wondered where Benjamin was.

She dreamed she was water. It oozed out of every pore and orifice until she was all water. A true India Lake.

Swans floated on her.

THE NEXT MORNING, the sun was out. India got dressed and went outdoors. She glanced toward the Strands. The water level had dropped dramatically so that it was only flooding up the boat ramp about ten feet. The water in India's own backyard was gone. The river was beginning to take her shape again after a week or more of feasting.

Jack drove up as India walked toward the pond. He parked his truck and ran to join her.

"Hello," he said. "How are you doing?"

"I think we survived it," she said.

The swans were gone again. The pond had returned to its shape, too. The river had receded.

"How's the rest of the refuge?" India asked.

"Things are drying out," he said. "Most of the swans went to Ridgefield."

She nodded. They continued walking down the path. The sun felt good. It was almost too warm for January. India squinted and looked toward the marsh. The top fence was clear of water. The bottom fence was clear of water, too, but something was caught on the barbed wire strands. India hated all the debris left after a flood. She put her hand over her eyes and peered at the fence. That wasn't debris. She opened the gate and ran toward the bottom fence.

"India," Jack called.

It was not debris. It was white. It was a white bird. A dead white bird. Contorted in death. Wings spread wide. Long neck twisted. A swan. A swan with a gray neck and head.

India screamed.

"India!" Jack called.

India sobbed as she stopped and faced the dead swan crucified on the barbed wire.

"India." Jack was next to her. "It's OK. I'll take care of it."

"I told you this was a mistake," she cried, turning on him. "Goddamned barbed wire. Trying to master nature. What bullshit."

She ran up the hill and down the path toward the road. She ran into the garage, threw open cupboards and tool boxes until she found what she wanted: wire cutters.

She ran toward the meadow again. Fury pumped her legs until she got to the first long expanse of barbed wire fence. She put the wire between the metal lips of the wire cutter and squeezed.

"Here's what I think about taming nature," she said.

"Hey! India! You're going to get hurt."

The wire gave, snapped, and whipped away from India in several directions. Jack jumped back. India went to the fence post: one, two, the wires were cut, jerking away once they were free, like metal snakes looking for earth.

"This is a stupid fence anyway, Jack," India said, hurrying to the next expanse of wire. "It doesn't keep the cows in. It's like some stupid political statement that means absolutely nothing: See, we put up fences even though they don't do any fucking good because the cows go through them like they were air." She followed the line of wire down further. "They kill wildlife, Jack. Makes me sick." She put the wire between the lips of the wire cutter. Squeezed. Metal gave way. To the cottonwood. She sliced the metal again and again.

"The rancher is the goddamned sheriff," Jack said, following her. "I sympathize with you, but he'll put you in jail. This is government land."

She looked at Jack. "Those fucking cows do more damage to this land than I could ever do. You are supposed to be protecting this land. You are supposed to be protecting the swans. This is a goddamned bird refuge!"

India cut the last wire on the north end of the marsh. She looked up and down where the fence had been. Now only fence posts and openness. India wiped her tears and went down to the second fence—to the dead swan. Jack followed her.

"Give me your gloves," she said.

He pulled his work gloves from his back pocket. India took the gloves and handed Jack the wire cutters.

She carefully unwrapped the swan from the fence, one wing at a time. Tears ran down her face. She held onto the body and carefully pulled the neck out of the barb.

Then the bird was in her arms. She was not as heavy as India thought she would be. It was almost like holding an infant. She took the cutters from Jack. Holding the swan carefully with one hand, she put the wire in the jaws of the cutter and squeezed.

"Here it ends," she said as the metal broke in two and whipped away from her.

She turned away from Jack and carried the swan toward home.

"They're going to find out about this," Jack called.

"They can all go fuck themselves," she murmured through her tears.

When she got home, she carefully held the swan under her outdoor faucet and gently rinsed her off. Then she lay her on the cement front porch. India got a towel and dried the bird off. The swan was still beautiful. Her bill was hard and black, her legs black, her feathers soft.

India's chest and throat hurt. She wanted to wail. Scream. She wanted to *do* something.

"I'm so sorry for your death," India said. "I will make certain you are honored."

Gently India pulled out a feather. Tears streamed down her face and onto her hands. She pulled out another feather. And another. The sun beat down on her. The dead bird lay before her. India knew this was right. Not that the bird was dead. But that she should take the feathers. When the clouds covered the sun, she knew she was finished.

India wrapped the swan in the towel and carried her back to the meadow. She walked to the middle of the field where the old bleached deer bones still rested. There she lay the swan onto the ground for the scavengers to feast upon. She stroked the swan's soft neck.

"Peace," she whispered.

Then she turned and walked away.

India put the feathers into a paper sack. Then she sat in her living room waiting for the police to come.

When they did not arrive, she fell to sleep.

"India, India," Benjamin's voice.

India opened her eyes. Benjamin leaned over her. Jack stood behind him.

"Are you all right?" Benjamin asked.

India sat up.

"What are you doing here?" India asked.

"I wanted to make sure you were all right," Benjamin said. "It's still a mess out there."

"Are the police outside to arrest me for vandalism?" India asked, looking at Jack.

He shook his head. "No, Indy. Everything's all right."

She closed her eyes. How she loved the sound of a patronizing voice.

"India, we have to talk," Benjamin said.

She opened her eyes.

"I don't want to," she said.

She looked at Benjamin. She saw the concern in his eyes, but she felt cold toward him. She didn't even feel angry. She recognized this feeling. Emily Dickinson called it "that formal feeling," although Emily had been talking about death. India felt formal, too.

"Jack told me what happened," Benjamin said. "With the swan."

She stared at him. "It was the swan you said reminded you of me. She's the one who's dead. I'm so tired. I'm tired of living in a world where so many of you don't get it."

"I'll be outside," Jack said. "I'll let you two talk."

"No," India said, standing. "I have nothing to say. I'd

like you both to leave."

Benjamin pulled a piece of paper from his jacket pocket. "I'll leave this with you then. It's legal. It's irrevocable." He held it out to her.

India took it and tried to read it. "What is it?"

"It says that the Dutch property, when transferred to Aviary Lumber, will forever be held in trust and will never be developed. We will keep it forever as a wilderness."

"It's not a wilderness now," India said. "It's just a strip of land left over after all the shits in the world destroyed or developed everything else."

"Well, it's a strip of land you love and it is now legally protected. You are the designated manager. I got an Aviary board meeting called, and my dad went in and read them the riot act. My brother is out on his ass until he can learn a little integrity."

"So you didn't know what the company was doing?"

Benjamin shook his head. "Of course not. You should have believed in me, India. I was surprised when I went to the meeting and saw my brother. I didn't know they were planning on acquiring this land. And when he asked me to spy on you—in order to get me back into the family fold, so to speak—I told him to go fuck himself. You should have known what we had was real. But you always doubted us. Doubted my love for you."

India's hand began to shake. Had she gotten everything wrong?

Jack looked away from her.

"I'm sorry," she said. "I—I don't know what to say.

I shouldn't have accused you. But you should have told me."

Benjamin looked into her eyes. She saw no love there this time.

"You have been unjustly accused too many times," India said.

"Yes," he said. "I wanted to give this to you. And to make sure you were safe. I'll get the rest of my things later. I will be in the area for a while to finish up my work with the swans, but I will only be here when you are not. Maybe we can complete our work on *Swans in Winter* separately. You can put the book together without me. You have more expertise in that area. If you can't do it alone, then just let it go. I'm no longer interested." He cleared his throat. "Goodbye, India Lake."

Benjamin walked out of the house.

Jack looked at her. "He just came rushing here through landslides and flood and who knows what else to see if you were all right. Aren't you going to go after him?"

She shook her head.

Jack made a noise; then he left, too.

India began to cry.

She got the bag of feathers and an old ivory cardigan. She poked the feathers through the sweater and tied them loosely together on the inside. She put it on over her shirt and looked in the mirror. Was this her swan cloak?

She took it off and hung it on the chair in her bedroom.

She smoothed the feathers down with her hand.

What had happened?

She may have gotten her swan cloak back but she had used it to fly right into a brick wall.

She turned off the light and went to bed.

Chapter Eighteen

THE SWANS FLEW back to the pond in the morning. The river had nearly returned to its original banks.

India went outside and stood near the swans. She did not spook them. They looked her way, then another way. Was she now one of them? She wished she could tell their story. She couldn't. She was not one of them.

Still.

She went to the house and got a yellow pad. Then she came back outside and leaned against the old cottonwood, and began to write:

Swan Maidens

I dream of swans. They wing their way through my sleep,

some white, some black, murmuring a truth I cannot yet decipher.

When I awaken I wonder what it is they symbolize.

I read about them. I learn their mating habits. How long their wingspans are. I watch them to learn their living habits. They float. They eat. They breathe. They are in each other's company constantly. This is what swans do in winter.

I read stories about swans. For the Greeks, the swan was a solar symbol, related to Apollo who is a decidedly male god. To the Slavs and Persians, the swan was a lunar symbol. The People of the Yenisei Basin in Mongolia believed swans menstruated like women: decidedly female. In some stories the swan was a transmutation of the Sun and the Moon: therefore the swan was a hermaphrodite. In other myths, the swan is the embodiment of Desire, male or female.

I know that swans are magnificent birds. They lift off from water with barely a sound. They dig around in mud all day, yet they do it with grace and aplomb. They talk to each other for hours, delicate coos of ohoooh, ohhhoooh. For hours they are silent.

I recall the story of the swan maidens. A version of this story exists in many cultures, although it may have originated in Siberia. The point of view of the story is usually male. A hunter stumbles upon six (or 9 or 11) women dancing in and around a lake in the wild. He sees their discarded garments in the grass: cloaks made from swan feathers. The hunter creeps down to the shore and steals one of the cloaks. Soon the women prepare to leave. They search for their sister's cloak but cannot find it. They finally tell her that they must leave and she is on her own. They each throw on their cloaks; as they do so, they transform into swans and fly away.

It is then that the hunter steps forward and tells the woman he has her cloak. He will not return it, but he begs her to marry him and promises to make her happy. She has to agree; it is the only possible way to retrieve the cloak. They return to his home and marry.

I have always wondered if she looked for her cloak every day. Did she lay in bed plotting how she would find it? I would have.

Wouldn't I?

The Swan Maiden has babies and lives many years with her husband. Does she slowly forget who and what she is? One of her children, most often a little girl, stumbles upon the cloak one day when she is feeling adventurous and wild, exploring a place in the house her father warned her against. The girl immediately takes the cloak to her mother. "Is this what you have longed for mother?" the child asks. "Is this what you have needed?" The woman exclaims in delight. Without a backward glance, she puts on her cloak, transforms into a swan, and flies away home.

The story does not end there. The hunter goes on a perilous journey to find his wife and bring her back home. Her father, the king, agrees the hunter can "have" the Swan Maiden if he can tell her apart from all of her other swan sisters. The hunter can and does, and he takes her back home where they reportedly live happily ever after.

I have never liked that ending. Storytellers warn against tampering with the elements of an old story. They are mythic. Time tested. All the pieces are symbolic and essential.

Or are they part of the propaganda that keeps us in our place? Is that too harsh an assessment? I don't like the ending of Swan Maiden. I do not believe it is a story about kings and hunters and babies and living happily ever after.

Isn't it a story about losing one's soul and finding it again? To the Celts the swan symbolized the soul. When the Swan Maidens came out of the sky to frolic along the shores of that lake in the wilds, why did they change from swans to women? Were they transforming from the wild to the tame? Or the tame to the wild?

And why did they leave a part of themselves vulnerable to theft? Was it a coincidence that a hunter is the thief? What part of us does that cloak represent?

Is it the part we take for granted, that part we don't even realize is essential for our being until it is gone? Do we lose it when we fall in love and give up "that part" to be obliging? Is that what happened to the Swan Maiden? She decided she had to compromise. Why didn't she just roar and go after the hunter and take back that cloak? Why did she agree to the half life the hunter offered? How could she? Because she has lost her cloak does she look at that hunter and believe he is her lost soul mate?

In the story, it turns out the cloak was always within her reach. It was hidden in her own home. Found by her own child. Is that it? Do we have to be childlike again to retrieve our lost souls? Do we have to become our wild adventurous child selves?

When we can do that—become innocent again—we find that which we have lost or carelessly thrown away. We know who we are again. We are whole and wholly ourselves.

Are swans then symbols of our true nature? Our souls? Desire? In the Arthurian legends, a Swan Knight roamed the wilderness looking for those women who had lost their way in the new world order. He looked for women who could not adjust to living in a "man's world." He was supposed to do whatever he could to make them happy again. I wonder if he succeeded. Could he change the world for them? And why was he the swan knight? Is there something about swans that can help us live in a world that does not always feel like our own?

From my spot near my home where I study the swans, I see one stretch her wings wide. I do the same. I hear my bones crack. Does she feel the same kind of relief I do from a kink in her lovely curved neck?

One day, the river where I live floods. Ponds become lakes, lakes rivers. Oceans. People talk into news cameras and point out the destructive power of Mother Nature. When the flood retreats, I find a dead swan caught on a barbed wire fence. I hold her in my arms, and I know then that she and hers are not symbols for anything. She was a wild creature, and now she is dead.

Wild is what I love. People are afraid of the wild. Even the word. Wild, to them, means something is out of control. To me, wild is natural. Wild equals nature. My passion is for the wild. For Nature. I ache for her embrace. I long to press my sole against her. When the swan died on that barbed wire fence, part of the wild died.

We need the wild. As a civilization we have lost our cloak of swan feathers: that part of our soul that keeps us wild. When part of nature and the Wild are lost, parts of ourselves are lost, too.

I am making swans a symbol again, aren't I? I don't mean to. Swans stand on their own. They have their own place in the cosmos separate from us. They have become part of our mythology. Have we become part of theirs? Maybe. They fly away every time we come near. Do they know we are looking for our lost souls? If they aren't careful we will take theirs instead and fashion them into cloaks of feathers we wear when we have forgotten who we really are—when we have forgotten who our true soul mate is.

I watch the swans. They are whole and wholly themselves, it seems, yet part of a community. They preen and cuddle and eat. I gaze at their wildness and I dance. I feel myself move in ways I have not moved before. I feel desires I have not known before.

I watch the swans and realize we cannot find our lost souls or soul mates in a cloak of feathers or in someone else's arms.

What the Swan Maiden lost when the hunter stole her cloak was her knowledge of her self. When the child returns the cloak to her, she is reunited with her self: with her own needs, desires, passions.

How many of us forget what we need or want? How

many of us compromise our dreams away? How many of us stop letting our voices be heard?

It is enough that the swans exist. For me, the swans are a reminder to be my true self, to hold my cloak of swan feathers close. That isn't their purpose, however. Swans exist in the wild as part of Nature. That is enough. They need no other reason.

INDIA FINISHED HER essay as it was beginning to get dark. She pressed her back against the cottonwood and held the yellow pad to her chest. She smiled. It was good to be able to tell her stories again.

She went back to the house to eat. Nancy had left a message that the county commissioners were meeting the next day to talk about POOL and the calendar. Nancy said she called all of the "Natural Women" and they were going to try to come. 10:00 a.m.

India laughed when she listened to the message. This was going to be fun. She typed up the Swan Maidens essay and then went to bed.

In the morning India plucked thirteen feathers from her cloak and put them in her bag along with a copy of the Swan Maidens essay. She drove to Rhonda's and picked her up. They drove to town and met the other POOLers in the commissioners' meeting room. India gave each of the Natural Women a long white feather.

"Sisters, POOLers, Natural women, Swan Maidens all," India said. "I'm sick of wasting my energy on these people."

"Hear, hear," Nancy said.

"So let's make it clear who we listen to," India said, "and it's not these people." She motioned to the empty commissioners' chairs.

The three commissioners filed into the room at 10:00. They conducted regular business for several minutes. Under new business, Dick Lament spoke up, "Several members of the community asked if we, the commissioners, as representatives of Shahalla County, would officially condemn the actions of the so-called POOLers."

"Excuse me," India said. She held a swan feather in her left hand as she stood.

"It's not time for you yet," Commissioner Cowers said.

"Yes, it is," India said. "We know you are doing this because of the lawsuit. You want to threaten us, to try to humiliate us, so that we'll back down. You've been trying to discredit us for years. We remind you we have more than seven hundred years of wisdom between us. We ain't backing down. But we also aren't giving you any more of our time or attention. We aren't going to try to change your minds. We're going to let our lawyer do the talking. We have the power now and we're going to use it. Good day, commissioners."

India stuck the feather into her hair, turned and left the room. She glanced behind her as the POOLers each put a feather in their hair or hats and followed India into the hallway. Once they were all together and outside the room, they laughed.

Marian held her feather in the air and said, "In defense of Mother Earth."

The other women held their feathers up high and yelled after her, "In defense of Mother Earth!"

BENJAMIN WAS IN the swan meadow when India returned. Her stomach lurched. She breathed deeply. She could walk into the house right now and probably never see Benjamin again. Her life would eventually settle back into what it had been before she met him.

Or she could go into the meadow and face him.

She took the copy of the Swan Maiden from her bag and walked toward Benjamin.

"Hey, Benjamin Swan," she said when she was a few feet from him.

Benjamin turned and looked at her just as he had from the very beginning. He saw her. He really saw people.

Did she see him?

Her knees wobbled.

"Hello, India Lake," he said.

"I wrote this," she said, handing him the pages. "For the book. I wanted to make certain it was OK with you."

"Thanks," he said. "I'll read it."

He turned back to the water and the swans.

India looked at his back for a moment. She nodded. She understood. She had betrayed him. That was not easy to forgive. She walked back toward the house.

"Have a good life, Benjamin Swan," she whispered.

Chapter Nineteen

"ALL RIGHT, ALL right," Nancy said. "Shaddup, allaya! Let's get this meeting started before January ends."

The POOLers lounged around India's kitchen table, on her couch, chairs, and floor. India leaned against the chair Beth sat in.

"Except for twenty-five copies we saved for posterity," Nancy said, "the Natural Women calendar is officially sold out!"

The women cheered. India laughed.

"We haven't gotten all of our accounts paid in full, but most of them are or will make good on it. After expenses, we will have over $25,000!"

This time the women roared. They jumped to their feet and embraced one another.

"Now," Nancy said, motioning with her hands for them to sit. "As you all know, we are very grateful to our photographer, Benjamin Swan, for his participation in this project. His artistry, gentleness, good humor, and talent at pornography were very much appreciated."

India looked at her hands.

"Anyway, in appreciation of all of that, we got him a little something. However. As you all know, there was a misunderstanding of sorts, and he is not here. He was invited but as you can see, he's not here. We wanted you all to see what we got him."

Deborah picked up a box. She lifted the lid and pulled out a black varsity jacket. She held it up for everyone to see. On the upper left arm sleeve was a white swan applique. On the right were the small letters POOL. She turned the jacket around. On the back were the words, in white, "Swan Knight."

India swallowed hard. She wanted to cry. Deborah carefully put the coat back into the box and put on the lid again.

"OK. Now," Nancy said. "We have another in our midst we want to honor. She is the person responsible for this whole crazy mess. Our fearless idea person. The woman who laughs in the face of Dick Lament. The woman who breaks down barriers—especially wire ones. Our own India Lake."

Whistles and cheers.

Deborah handed a box to Anna who passed it across to Beth who gave it to India.

India stood up and lifted the lid from the box. She

pulled out a white varsity jacket. Except it was more than white. She smoothed her hand across the soft fabric. It felt like down, but it wasn't. The seamstress had used stitching to create the illusion of feathers. The trim on the ends of the sleeves, the collar, shoulders, and bottom of the jacket were black. On the left shoulder was an applique of a long black rose. On the right was the word POOL. India turned the jacket around. On the back, in black lettering, were the words: Swan Maiden.

"Oooh, oooh," India said.

"Put it on," the women called.

Beth took the jacket from India and held it open for her. India turned around and put her arms in the sleeves. Beth dropped the jacket onto her shoulders. India blinked away the tears.

"Thank you, India. Thank you for your determination," Nancy said. "We all read your essay. That's where we got the idea for these jackets. And we liked your jacket so much we all decided to get one, too."

Deborah went out the front door and began bringing boxes inside the house.

"Clemmy," Nancy called as she handed out the boxes. "Pansy."

Soon all of the women had on their jackets.

India laughed. Thirteen Swan Maidens.

"What a beautiful picture," Nancy said. "I wish I had a camera. Or a photographer. Oh wait. He was accused of something he didn't do so now he's gone."

The room became suddenly silent. The women looked at India. She stared back at them.

The party broke up soon after. Exhausted, India picked up and did the dishes. As she was turning off the lights, she noticed a box leaning up against a chair. She picked it up. One of the women had left behind her jacket. India opened the box and pulled out the Swan Knight jacket. She pressed it against her face, quickly, then let it drop back into the box.

She switched off the lights and went to bed.

AT THE BEGINNING of February, India returned to work. She knew she had some fences to mend. She would do it. She wasn't certain how much longer she wanted to stay at the library, but for now, it was her job. She still had to figure out how her library job would fit into her management of Turtle Pond and the surrounding land. It would all fall into place over time, she was certain.

On her first day back at the library, the staff waited for her in the back room. On her desk was a cake in the shape of a naked woman.

India laughed so hard she nearly cried.

"Next time," Teri said. "Would it hurt to ask us to get naked, too?"

Jack came into the library that morning.

"Hello," she said.

"Hello, India," Jack said. "How's your first day back? Anyone bothering you?"

"Only you," India said. She smiled.

"Are you OK?" he asked.

She nodded.

"Benjamin is returning to Mott," Jack said. "I thought

you'd want to know."

So there it was. She and Benjamin were truly finished. It was over.

"The POOLers got a gift for Benjamin," India said. "If I bring it to you, can you send it to him?"

"Sure," Jack said.

She shook her head. "I know I blew it all around, Jack. I blew it with you. Then I blew it with Benjamin. I managed to do the one thing I could do to alienate him. I was just as stupid as all those people who accused him of taking those pictures of that girl. I'm so sorry."

"Yes, you are."

India laughed. "You are a good man, Jack Combs."

"You want to go to lunch?" he asked.

"Thanks. Not today."

"OK. We'll see you, India."

Every day India went to Turtle Pond and watched the swans. It was strange not to see Benjamin there. Not to feel his presence anywhere. She wondered if she would ever get used to it.

Violet resumed her belly dance class. POOL gave Daniel Salmonson a check for $10,000. Ten days later, he filed papers with the county stating his intention to bring about a class action lawsuit on behalf of the women of POOL. Three days later, Andrew Stephenson and Daniel Salmonson brokered a deal. The county had been sued twice in three years. Their insurance carrier urged them to negotiate. The county agreed to a community advisory committee made up of three POOL members and two county employers. Within thirty days, the committee would recommend who to hire as a qualified Integrated Vegetation and Pest Management consultant. This consultant would devise procedures and policies for a true IVPM program with the goal of eliminating the use of all chemical pesticides within the next three years. The county wanted the women to sign away their rights to ever sue. The women refused. The county folded.

At the victory party, Daniel Salmonson returned $8,000 of POOL's retainer. India told the press—which Nancy had thoughtfully notified—that Shahalla County would soon become a leader in environmental protection.

"People are so discouraged," India said. "They hear one awful news story after another about the environment, and they feel they can't do anything. But here's the thing: if everyone took care of one small piece of land and was cognizant of that piece's place in the scheme of things, pollution would end." She snapped her fingers. "Just like that. If everyone looked at Nature as a part of themselves, if they protected that piece of land as if it were their own arm, they wouldn't let anyone pour toxic chemicals into their arm, wouldn't let anyone pollute the bloodstream of that arm, wouldn't let that arm be cut off from their fingers, their shoulder, their heart. Pollution would end overnight practically. Shahalla County, which so wisely protected Sasquatch thirty years, ago is now taking the logical next step toward protecting all of the environment, including us humans."

"Will you all get naked next year?" a reporter asked. "In defense of Mother Earth?"

The women laughed. Almost as one, they pulled their swan feathers from the pocket of their Swan Maiden jackets and held them aloft. "In defense of Mother Earth!" they cried.

THE POOLERS DECIDED to use the money they earned to start a pilot environmental education program to take around to the schools.

India put together *Swans in Winter* and began sending it out. Three Pacific Northwest publishers were interested, particularly after they found out Benjamin was the photographer and India the instigator of the Natural Women calendar.

India started sending out her novels again, too. In her cover letter, she mentioned her involvement in the Natural Women calendar. She began getting ideas for new novels. Especially one about a woman who spends the winter watching the swans.

CHAPTER TWENTY

ONE DAY, JACK called India at work.

"Hey, Indy," he said. "I'm going to see Benjamin this weekend. I can take that gift to him from the POOLers if you want. I'm leaving in a half-hour."

"Thanks for the notice," she said. "My lunch break is coming up. I'll go home and get it."

"I'll meet you there," Jack said, "in about twenty minutes?"

"See you then."

India drove home. It was a beautiful February day. The sun was out. A few clouds moved in the gorge. India went into her house and got the jacket and box from her closet. She carried the box out to the living room and stood with it as she looked out the window at Turtle

Pond. The swans floated gracefully on the water.

Someone stood a short distance from them.

Benjamin.

India hesitated only a moment before taking the jacket out of the box and going outside with it. She walked down the path toward Benjamin.

Her stomach lurched. He was so beautiful.

She loved him.

She had told him he did not have to be the Swan Knight with her. He could be himself. Yet she had never really believed in him. In them.

"Hello," she said when she was a few feet from him.

He turned around, startled. His eyes registered pain when he looked at her. She flinched.

"I thought you were at work," he said.

"I didn't see your truck," she said.

"It's at Rhonda and Isaac's," he said. "I stopped by for a visit and a last look. Jack was supposed to come by."

"Ahhh, Jack. I think he set this up. He called me and asked me to come home right away. He was going to pick up this to take to you. It's a gift from the POOLers."

She held out the jacket to Benjamin. He took it and looked at it.

"Wow," he said, his fingers resting on the letters S and W in Swan Knight. "This is incredible."

"Put it on," India said.

Benjamin shrugged off his coat, hesitated, then handed it to India. He put on the Swan Knight jacket.

"Fits nice," he said.

"It looks great," India said.

They were silent for a moment.

"I thought you went back to Mott," she said.

"I did. For a week. Just to see if I could do it. I did. No one accused me of doing anything wrong." He looked away from her. "Do I have that kind of face, India, that people accuse me of such terrible things?"

"Oh, no, Benjamin. You're a nice man. I guess us cynics have a difficult time believing in nice men. I'm *so* sorry I accused you. I was wrong. It was a terrible thing to do."

"I should have told you everything as soon as I knew my family was involved," he said. "I was afraid you wouldn't want me any more if you knew my family owned a lumber company."

"Am I really that fanatical?" India asked.

"You are formidable," he said.

"I won't apologize for that," she said.

"I never asked you to," he said.

She looked at her feet.

"I got scared, Benjamin. I didn't mean to drive you off. I loved you. I still do. I love you like I love this place."

Benjamin looked at her with tears in his eyes. "Swans mate for life," he said. "At least this one does."

India's heart raced.

Benjamin opened his arms. He reminded India of one of the swan's stretching out his wings—waiting for the embrace. India went to him, and they held each other for a long while.

"I loved *Swans in Winter*, by the way," Benjamin said.

"Did you show it to Rhonda? She will be so impressed you figured out who your soul mate is."

"You mean my own sweet wonderful self?" she asked.

He kissed her mouth.

She looked up at him. "Will you stay with me and be my love?"

"I will," he said. "I want to make love to you right here and now."

"Too much goose shit," she said.

He laughed. They watched the swans. About thirty of them floated on the pond.

"They're all growing up," Benjamin said.

India nodded. "They'll be flying home soon. Maybe we'll do the sequel to *Swans in Winter* some day."

"*Swans in Summer*?"

"Exactly," India said. "I've always wanted to go to Alaska."

"Me, too," Benjamin said.

India took Benjamin's hand. It was cold in hers. She rubbed it, kissed it, then laced her fingers with his.

Suddenly the swans lifted up from the pond. Silently. Leaving barely a ripple in the water.

India and Benjamin watched the sky as the swans curved toward the river, and then curved back toward India and Benjamin, flying in an S shape. India laughed and waved. Benjamin did the same.

"Be safe! Be wild!" India called.

"I don't think you can do both all of the time," Benjamin said.

"Do what?"

"Be safe and still be wild," he said.

They watched the sky until the swans and clouds melted into each other.

The swans were gone for another year.

India heard a cry.

She looked around.

"That was an eagle," she said.

She looked up.

A bald eagle flew above them and over to the camouflage of the tall evergreens.

"The eagles are back," India said, grinning.

"What would you choose?" Benjamin asked. "To be safe or to be wild?"

"Both," India said. "If I couldn't have both? I'd chose the wild."

Benjamin held out his hand. India took it and danced beneath it, moving her hips in a figure eight. She twirled and danced, creating sacred shapes with her body. She closed her eyes. She *was* the sacred shape. Creating a universe with every breath. Dancing for the bald eagle and heron and wind and rain.

When she opened her eyes, she saw Benjamin watching her. She grinned. Benjamin picked her up and whirled her around.

"This I love," he said.

Summer Equinox Under a Nearly Full Moon

THE THIRTEEN WOMEN danced under the moon. Cows watched them from another pasture, leaning their heads over the new wooden fences. Coyotes howled in the distance.

India knew Benjamin was taking pictures—they all knew—but she could not tell where he was. They danced under the full moon just as they had six months earlier, only this time, it was warmer outside. Some of the women were fully naked, some fully clothed, some in-between. India left on her boots. Too much cow shit.

After a time, the women stopped dancing and put on their clothes. Benjamin came and stood with them as they prepared to return to their cars.

"Here's to the beginning of Natural Women 2," Nancy said.

"I can't believe we did this in December," Anna said. "It's cold *now*."

The women started walking back.

"Do you think anyone saw us here tonight?" Gina asked.

"They'll just think we're a coven of witches," Clementine said.

"What is the rest of that round?" Nancy asked. "We are the witches back from the dead. . ."

"Perhaps this time we could all be a different wild animal," Marian said.

"Then we wouldn't be naked," Clementine said.

"We don't have to be naked," Beth said. "We're Natural Women, not naked women."

Benjamin put his hand on India's arm to keep her from leaving with the others.

The women continued walking, the moonlight following them.

"How about a swim in my pool?" Cheryl asked.

"Oh yes," Rhonda said. "That would be delightful. Sans clothes?"

"Of course," Cheryl said.

"I have a surprise for you," Benjamin said to India. He took her hand and led her toward the evergreen woods. As they got closer she saw a tent at the edge of the forest.

India laughed.

"I thought about spreading a blanket out under the moonlight but you might have a better chance of actually sleeping inside a tent away from bugs and cow shit." Benjamin opened the flap. "After you, my love."

India took off her shoes, then went into the tent. Benjamin followed. "I've got food and water," he said.

India kissed his mouth.

"I just want you," she said.

They made love with the moonlight coming through the walls of the tent, creating a milky blue light. India felt the ground beneath the sleeping bag as Benjamin moved deep inside of her. She hoped the coyotes heard her cries of pleasure.

They fell to sleep in each other's arms. India awakened soon after; she was very cold. She hurriedly put on her clothes. And coat.

"You cold?" Benjamin asked sleepily.

"Shh," India said. "It's OK. Sleep."

She tucked the sleeping bag around him and slipped out of the tent into the moonlit night. She rubbed her arms and started walking toward the Seven Sisters. The gorge cliffs were stone pieces of shadow and shady moonlight. She wondered if Sasquatch wandered those sloping inaccessible mountain forests tonight. In the arctic, she realized, the swans slept under this same full moon.

India reached the seven trees. She hugged one of them. Then she let go and twirled around, her arms open, taking in the entire gorge, the moon, stars, trees, ground, and naked Benjamin who just stepped out of the tent and was looking around for her. She tilted her head back and opened her arms wider.

She called out, "This I love!"

ABOUT THE AUTHOR

KIM ANTIEAU HAS written many novels, short stories, poems, and essays. Her work has appeared in numerous publications, both in print and online, including *The Magazine of Fantasy and Science Fiction, Asimov's SF, The Clinton Street Quarterly, The Journal of Mythic Arts, EarthFirst!, Alternet, Sage Woman,* and *Alfred Hitchcock's Mystery Magazine.* She was the founder, editor, and publisher of *Daughters of Nyx: A Magazine of Goddess Stories, Mythmaking, and Fairy Tales.* Her work has twice been short-listed for the Tiptree Award and has appeared in many best-of-the-year anthologies. Critics have admired her "literary fearlessness" and her vivid language and imagination. John Clute, writing about her novel *The Gaia Websters* in the third edition of *The Science Fiction Encyclopedia,* had this to say: "In the end, as usual in her work, any useful answers are held by the Earth herself." Clute's words could serve as a handy description of Kim's writing and her life. Kim's first novel *The Jigsaw Woman* is a modern classic of feminist literature. Her other novels include *Church of the Old Mermaids, The Fish Wife, Ruby's Imagine, Her Frozen Wild,* and *Mercy, Unbound.* Kim lives in the Pacific Northwest with her husband, writer Mario Milosevic. Learn more about Kim and her writing at www.kimantieau.com.

Made in the USA
Charleston, SC
30 June 2012